BURSKA'S SPIDER KING

(Book 3 of the Spider Hopping Series)

The Spider Hopping Series starts with *Aliens and Spiders.*

K.S. Riggin

Table of Contents

Chapter One
A Brief Summary and Reminder

Caralee

It all started when the aliens came. When Danuel, the delivery guy, who also happened to be my future computer list-assigned mate, brought our groceries, I was babysitting my little sister, Lissie. I'd lost her and was searching for the herd of spiders she'd let out of the fenced-in area. I was also hunting for the mischievous toddler who loved to hide. Danuel offered to help. That was all good until space ships landed and spider-like aliens started climbing out of them. We finally found Lissie, and in fear for our lives, the three of us fled into the woods.

It was lucky that we found a niche that held food, water, and shelter, but the aliens caught up with us. They captured Lissie and me in huge spider webs. Then they shot Danuel with some kind of sleeping bullet. We all woke up on their alien ship, separated into different rooms.

At last, we were shoveled back together in one room and supposedly trained to be mediators. I'm not sure that worked really well, but the alternative didn't look promising. The aliens finally released us to live like primitives, except with added rules. Then they demanded that Danuel and I get married.

Danuel is a great guy, and I fell in love with him, so that was all good, and so was little Miguel, who I gave birth to, but then my dad's ship landed from his year away on planet exploration. We discovered that everyone in the city was in stasis, frozen in a standing position like fence posts.

We woke Dad, but that didn't go well since he became ballistic over Danuel and me having a baby. Dad was put back into stasis. We tried waking up Mom next. We hoped she could tone down Dad's fury.

But Planet Burska, who is sentient, is very demanding. She wanted Danuel and me to turn all humans into cavemen, or else she was going to do something dire with them. So, no pressure on us or anything.

It's a good thing the herd spiders were on our side. I think that was because our son is the *Spider Hopper*, which is said like that's a super powerful position. Danuel and I still don't know what it means, except that the herd spiders listen to Miguel and sometimes even bow to him, even though he's only a baby. They said that Miguel talked to them and to the planet. But the baby can't talk to his father and me, other than *goo-goo* like other babies his age.

My four-year-old sister rides the biggest of the herd spiders, Koosk, who I think is the head herd spider. Lissie also communicates with the bald-headed, multi-eyed, sharp-toothed teacher alien named Dokófray, who is usually in charge of us.

It's all very confusing, but the worst part is that twenty-year-old Danuel and I, Caralee, aged sixteen, are supposed to teach all the adults to reformat their lives according to the dictates of the planet, Burska. Once we wake them all up, of course. Kind of a challenge, right?

Chapter Two

Danuel

Baby Miguel is again sound asleep. I'm not sure babies are supposed to sleep this much, but maybe it's because his life is so eventful. Herd spiders are constantly sauntering about. The alien, Dokófray, is usually arguing with little Lissie. Miguel's mother, my wife, is frequently in tears from frustration, and her mother, just newly awakened, is having a hard time holding on to reality.

So, if a little extra sleep is needed for Miguel to deal with the constant upheaval of his life, I think it's very understandable. Sometimes, I'd like to get covered up in a nice leafy blanket and sleep away life's complications. Like the big one coming up — waking up Lissie's father, who has already bellowed and thundered over my marriage with his far too young daughter, as he puts it, not to mention producing a baby in the process.

But Burska wants us to wake up five people, and so far, we've only successfully dealt with one. *Produce a calming environment*, Burska tells us, through her alien pal, Dokófray. As if. Aliens have invaded and thrown our lives in turmoil. *Restful resolution* might be workable inside a spaceship room, but with people, angry because they've been in stasis for a year. Those are the same adults who are supposed to be instructed on how to live on Burska by a couple of teenagers . . .

I'm starting to wish we could turn around and head back to our comfortable hut by the river. It may not have been fancy. In fact, what I'd labored over and built was worse than any hut I'd ever seen. It was unstable and entirely too prone to have leaks in a rainstorm, but at least it was quiet. Or it was until the herd of spiders descended and began worshipping and communing with baby Miguel. But that is a whole other problem that we'll have to deal with when we return.

~~~~~~~~~~

"Is the baby asleep?" Caralee asked as her herd spider brought her next to mine.

I nodded and looked down. Miguel's slow breathing and his lack of crying were obvious indicators. I knew that Caralee's question was just because she was missing the baby. She got anxious whenever she wasn't holding him. I nodded again, then flashed her a smile and sent an air kiss her way.

But half of my brain was thinking about what she'd just done. It was an impressive feat that she'd gotten a herd spider to respond to her wishes and cart her over to me. I never had any control over my herd spider 'horse". Most of the time, the one I was riding galloped off with me as a non-controlling passenger or stubbornly refused to go forward at all. Koosk urged them forward. He probably ordered them to carry me, too. Just call me Herd Spider Unpopular. I bet they drew straws. The loser had to be my beast of burden for the day.

"I *thought* the spider over here," my wife said. She showed me pictures through our *mind link*. Flashes of Miguel and me. If that was the secret, maybe I could do that. It was a hopeful thought, if a doubtful one.

"And your mom?"

Caralee sighed. "She's with Lissie, but she keeps forgetting things. She doesn't understand why Lissie and I look older and why Koosk is so big. She still keeps demanding to be reunited with her patients at the hospital."

"I don't understand why Koosk is humongous either," I said. "He's a male. He should be smaller than the females."

The herd spider I was riding made a noise. In a human, we'd called that a snort or a chuckle. Somewhere in between those two, I figured. Whichever, it was the sound of negation. That was extremely puzzling since herd spiders weren't supposed to understand our language. Yet Koosk seemed to, and the guy I was riding had just indicated that he was absorbing some of what we were saying. Mysteries surrounded us, each one more head-thumping and hair-pulling than the last.

"Form a *restive atmosphere*," Caralee quoted from one of the nonsensical training sessions we'd been forced to endure on the alien's ship.

She was kidding me, but there was truth in it Restoring calm was something I needed to work harder on. I would if things ever settled down around us. But there was always something new, something weird.

"How do you want to handle this waking up your dad thing?" I asked, focusing on our main obstacle going forward.

"Mom will handle that. Dokófray can turn off the stasis and leave our mom to do whatever she always does that soothes him. You know, a few kisses?" she said.

That's a soothing process?" I asked, lifting my eyebrows up and down in what I hoped was a suggestive manner.

Caralee laughed, which woke up Miguel. His mother's chuckles were always a magnet for Miguel's hunger. He fidgeted his body, opened his eyes wider, and squawked.

Immediately, every herd spider froze to a standstill, including the one I was riding. All eyes turned to Miguel.

Dokófray rode his herd spider close. "Ah, the young prince awakes," he said. He and Miguel did that thing where they stared eye-to-eye, well in Dokófray's case, it was probably his two principal eyes that stared eye-to-eye. But what was strangest is that Miguel, who had been on the brink of a full-out piercing wail, which was his demand to be passed to Caralee for his source of milk, was now quiet.

"Do you suppose this is a stretch break?" I asked, eager to step down and walk around a bit.

"I hope so, but Dad's ship is just over there," Caralee said, pointing to what was a mere mile or two away.

Lissie and their mother rode up then. Four-year-old Lissie, of course, was on Koosk. Her mother was on another herd spider, one I'd never seen before, but then the herd spiders all looked alike to me. Caralee was good at telling them a part, but I wasn't.

"Why are we stopping?" Lissie wanted to know, then, "Oh," she said, noticing the communications going on. "What are they saying, Koosk?"

"It would be nice to have Lissie's instant translator. I waited patiently to see if Caralee's little sister would feel like letting us in on the secret meeting happening right in front of us. Shouldn't being a father of the great Spider Hopper give me some special rights? Shouldn't being Lissie's brother-in-law give me a pipeline to what she was learning?

"Caralee, where are your clothes? Why are you wearing those shabby leaves?" their mother asked as if we hadn't already explained that to her four times.

The three of us shot a glance in her direction, then inhaled long, slow breaths – *a quick dose of patience,* Caralee called the practice.

My wife met my eyes and shrugged. "Burska doesn't like clothes like yours, Mom," Caralee told her mother again.

"Who is this Burska? Why is she telling you what to do?" her mother asked, getting rather huffy about it.

Lissie tuned back in. "Koosk says we need to spend the night here. He's sent for some fruit."

"I thought Burska was in a hurry to get this done," I questioned.

Lissie just rolled her eyes and dismounted. Caralee was climbing down, too. I figured there was no sense sitting a second more. I'd never call riding a herd spider a comfortable place to be.

"Thanks for the ride," I told my current herd spider, then patted him on the shoulder. I thought about giving him some pictures, but how do you flash a thank you?

The spider turned away and then sent an image. The orchard by the farm house? Dead fruit on the ground, a rope around one of his legs? Was this the spider I'd ridden that day? I wanted to confirm that, but he'd already galloped away. Still, it was a major breakthrough for me. I'd actually made contact.

"Mmmma," Miguel screamed, losing interest in communing with Dokófray.

That was Miguel's way of getting his needs satisfied. The baby wasn't into patience. It was right now, hurry, hurry or pay with your eardrums.

Caralee was already pulling the baby out of my arms, eager to hold him and cater to whatever he wanted.

She needs another, Dokófray sent into my mind.

"Another what?" I asked before I understood what he was suggesting. I blinked and stepped back. Yeah, that would make her parents real happy with me, not that I had any control over the possibility. It wasn't like Caralee, and I had any ability to practice abstinence.

Dokófray snickered and walked away. Whatever he'd been discussing with baby Miguel, he chose not to air it with me. Typical.

Lissie

Koosk didn't tell me everything. I felt it. He locked me out. Why? I never do that. I tell him everything.

Did Burska tell him to? Why? Didn't she want Daddy woke up? Did she change her mind?

Mommy was still acting funny. She kept forgetting things. Koosk said the fruit would help her, but she'd already eaten some. She wasn't any better.

We gave a fruit to Daddy, too. But Daddy still acted mean. What if Gorla fruit only worked on us borned on Burska?

I wanted to ask Dokófray, but he went away. Maybe back to his ship. He never sleeps with us. Maybe he doesn't trust us.

Mrs. Turner

I didn't understand why we were riding around the countryside on herd spiders when I needed to take care of my patients. I know the kids meant well, but I had responsibilities. I asked them about it again, but their faces got funny looks on them. Caralee never could hide anything from me, but something was up. I could tell.

Danuel kept holding someone's baby. Was he babysitting? Where was the child's mother? Danuel looked like he'd grown a lot. He looked more man than boy now. His arms and shoulders were massive. Of course that was one of those things we'd noticed on Beatnik. The planet seemed to enhance the physique of the males. It also made women more fertile. I wondered if I needed to have a talk with Caralee again. She and Danuel were getting too chummy. Maybe I should slip her some birth control.

But they'd taken me away from the hospital. I didn't wake up there. I woke up in, I think, the garbage dump. Why would I have been there?

Lissie, where has she gone? She is only three years old. She shouldn't be wondering around unsupervised. I must scold Caralee. Where is she? Caralee is holding that baby again. Whose is it? Is she babysitting that baby instead of Lissie?

"Cara," I called out.

"Do you need something?" Danuel asked.

He was such a nice boy/man. He would make a good husband for my Caralee. "Where is Lissie?" I asked. "Tell Caralee that she needs to find the child. Lissie's a baby, only three. She can't be running wild with all these herd spiders around. Some of them are males. Do they still have their claws?"

"Relax, Mrs. Turner," I said, patting her arm. "The girls are fine. Koosk is watching Lissie. She's four now, by the way. She had a birthday."

I scanned the area in search of my younger daughter. No luck. Wherever she'd gone, she wasn't in sight, but then, neither was that giant herd spider.

What had the boy said? I played it back, then shook my head. "That's not true, Danuel. I would know. I'm her mother. We have parties for birthdays. And cake. I tried to think if that had happened, but I couldn't remember.

It didn't matter. I needed to get back to my patients. They needed me. I hoped the doctors weren't looking for me. I didn't want to get in trouble. Of course, I never had before. My reviews as a nurse were always excellent.

But something was wrong. Why was I out in the woods and not at the hospital?

Danuel

Mrs. Turner was looking more and more upset. Where was that fruit we were promised? As if my thought had been heard, a young herd spider came trotting up to us, a bag of Gorla fruit in her hands. I took the bag and handed a fruit to Mrs. Turner.

"Oh, no. We can't eat these," she said. She eyed it a moment, then grabbed one and took a bite. "Well, I guess it can't hurt," she said, munching the rest of it.

I stood up and carried the fruit to my wife and son. Miguel was milk-satisfied and crawling about in the dirt. I handed a Gorla to Caralee, then took a bite of one for myself. I chewed for a moment and fingered some Gorla paste to Miguel. He gave me a big smile, then sucked my finger while making happy sounds. Any minute, he'd probably start singing, which would attract the whole herd.

I picked him up and finger-fed him some more of the fruit.

Dokófray suddenly appeared in front of me. Was he up to his tricks, even without the magic box that Lissie had buried?

"Burska say, Gorla not work on mother human."

Caralee gasped. She dropped her fruit, her eyes expanding into horror. "So what do we try? Is there some other root or fruit we can get her?"

"Burska tries to adapt to others. She works on it now. Miguel says give her a second, Gorla. Maybe that works."

I looked down at my son. If anyone else had said that Miguel could offer medical opinions, I'd laugh in their face, but on this planet, the impossible was our daily sustenance.

"Will you talk to me soon?" I asked my son, whispering into his tiny ear.

He looked at me and giggled, although I hadn't touched his belly or made a funny noise. His eyes stared into mine, deep green and serious. The giggle was gone at that moment as he studied me.

"He's sending pictures, Danuel," Caralee cried out, her face no longer a study in tragic but of wonder.

And then, I, too, caught what the baby was sending me. Flashes of me with the herd spiders, angry, ordering them out of the shed. Did I really look like that, my eyes full of demon lights, my face hard and threatening?

"That's not me," I told Miguel. "Or at least not the me I want to be, but I just don't understand everything that's happening. Why do the spiders keep gathering around, pushing your mother and me out?"

Miguel's eyes continued their piercing stare and deepened into the deep intensity that a baby might get from a new toy or his mother's breasts, I suppose. Then I saw other images: Lissie with Koosk, hugging him and sleeping beside him as Koosk tenderly gathered her up in his multiple spidery arms. Then Miguel showed me the old spider with Caralee when Miguel was about to arrive, the bite that had ended her pain and allowed her to laugh while giving birth.

Okay, I could see. I was holding back, refusing to allow their friendliness. I needed to invite the herd spiders into my . . . what my consciousness? My heart? Was Miguel telling me that the spiders were all like Koosk? Did I want that kind of relationship?

More pictures came flashing through my mind. Miguel is growing older. I see Miguel walking among the spiders, patting them, talking with them and enjoying their companionship. And where were Caralee and I? There. Caralee was sitting beside me, obviously growing another child, while a giant herd spider was playing with a toddler, a little boy, but not Miguel because this one had blonde hair and bright blue eyes with Caralee's nose and mouth and a look about him that let me know he was my son.

"So our role in this is just to make more children?" I asked Miguel, feeling irritated with the picture he'd sent.

"Fah, fah, fah," baby Miguel babbled out happily.

"Father?" I said, amazed that his muh for milk and mother had been exchanged for a new sound. Was he really trying to say, father? Why not daddy?

Another flash, this one with a wider scope. There were people spread across the sandy area where our hut was located. A whole village, in fact. Was that what this future Miguel was showing me would look like? Obviously, there would be a toddler and another on the way. But all those people, who were they? Why were they there?

"Fah fah," Miguel gurgled, and I saw the herd of spiders passing in and among the humans, helping, guiding, and loving. The children were hugging them and kissing the spiders, just like with Lissie and Koosk. Their parents were smiling, working on reed-sewn blankets and preparing meals in turtle bowls. Everyone was clothed as Caralee and I were in leafy shirts and skirts. Several were wearing hats from the corumba tree, the same leaf I used for Miguel's baby diapers.

"Fah," Miguel said again, looking completely satisfied with this series of images.

I glanced over at Caralee. It was obvious that she, too, was getting the projections. She was mouth-dropped in wonder, her eyes glowing.

I studied the latest image, scanning the faces. All young people, our peers, and presumably their children of varying ages. Where were the older people, the girls' parents and our former teachers, the people who'd run the government and make all the decisions? Perhaps they were in other villages?

Miguel's eyes grew wider, and he shook his head. Sadness? Loss? The images grew fuzzy then, and the village faded away until all the images were gone. With the show over, Miguel retreated back into babyhood.

"Goo," he said, and then he issued the slight body heave that I knew so well. It meant he'd dirtied his diaper. The stench hit my nose at the same moment that his action registered.

My eyes met Caralee. She laughed and then looked in the other direction. Ha! I knew what that meant. I chuckled to myself, then stood up to deal with the cleanup and a leaf change. I guess it was true that enlightenment always comes in short bursts.

Dokófray

So it has begun. Burska was right about Danuel. He was slow to learn and slower to agree, but I could see now that his brain was beginning to accept the way things would be. He had done well so far; although both Caralee and he suffered from instantaneous rage, a heritage from their ancestors, they were maturing well. There was still hope for them.

Little Miguel's ability was stunning. Burska was right to have such faith in this small bundle of humanity. Although Lissie, who was also a youngling, had amazed me at times, this was different. Miguel was the desired achievement. He would truly lead the way and become Burska's spider king. Progress.

Chapter Three

Caralee

The herd spiders brought a different kind of fruit to my mother. Danuel and I had never seen it before. We wondered why and what it was supposed to do for her, but we trusted Koosk and Dokófray enough to urge her to eat it.

Unfortunately, the next morning, we saw little difference in her behavior. She complained about being removed from the hospital, explained how her patients needed her and asked again whose baby I was holding. It was disheartening. Danuel said that maybe seeing my father might stabilize her. That was all I had to cling to.

My sister Lissie was not handling the situation with our mother well either. I'd seen her crying into Koosk's cephalothorax, several of his legs wrapping her into a secure position, a hug by all definitions. But this morning, when she came by to pick up a piece of fruit and sit with Mom, her eyes were still red.

Since I was already sitting beside Mom, Lissie came and gave me a kiss, a rarity. Of course, I kissed her back, but I didn't dare try to hold her as Koosk had done. I noticed that Danuel didn't do his usual either, which was to grab Lissie, turn her upside down, and cart her around in an upside-down position. This morning seemed too serious for that kind of frivolity.

We reached the landed ship, entered, and headed for the chamber where Dad stood in his angry pose. Mom reached out to him, crying.

I remembered then that she hadn't seen him for over a year. He'd been on a mission to find other planets for Earth's migration.

Danuel had thoughtfully delivered two chairs, one for Dad and one for Mom. But I doubted they would ever thank him for his thoughtfulness. It seemed that no matter what he did, he had become the evil seducer of my innocence. Mom, ignoring the chair Danuel brought her, continued to cling to her husband's stiff body.

Dokófray had to ask us to steer her over to the side so the alien could proceed with his magic trick of turning Dad back on. We were eager to hang back, none of us eager to have Dad initiate another stern lecture or launch into the angry venting of before.

Dad opened his eyes and saw Mom. She was embracing and kissing him. That part was nice to see. I was glad to see how much they still loved each other because my dad was returning every hug and kiss. But then, it looked like Dad was about to collapse. Danuel ran forward, grabbed Dad, and pushed him over to the chair. Mom finally sat down then, moving her chair even closer until her legs were touching Dad's.

I noticed that Danuel's quick dash wasn't even noticed by either of them. Happy to escape their notice, he returned to my side, leaving the couple still staring into each other's eyes in the way lovers do.

Meanwhile, Mom and Dad were holding hands and gushing I love you, and I missed you. It was going great until Dad asked, "How are the girls?"

And then it all came crashing down. Mom broke into tears and sobbed about how much we'd changed and how everything was weird.

"But are they okay?" Dad wanted to know, his face looking puzzled by Mom's strange breakdown.

Apparently, he had absolutely no recall of when we'd wakened him before. Were we going to be upbraided freshly? Didn't we get points for having already walked that stony path?

"Lissie, take them a couple of fruits," I said, whispering softly so that only she could hear.

She broke from Koosk's arm and arms to glance over at me. "Why don't you do it?" she wanted to know.

"Miguel?" I said, gesturing with my nose to the baby in my arms.

Of course, I knew I could have handed the baby to Danuel, but we'd tried that the first time. It made Dad angry. He'd smiled at Lissie before.

But presenting a couple of the fruits that we weren't supposed to eat was still dangerous. I supposed that Lissie was right to hesitate. I glanced at Dokófray, more or less asking his opinion since I knew he would have heard my whisper. Our alien could hear thoughts. Whispers must be as easy as breathing.

Dokófray shrugged.

Okay, so he was leaving this all up to us. I looked back at Lissie, wondering if she'd seen Dokófray's response. Whether she had or hadn't, she was already grabbing two fruits from our bag and heading for her parents.

"Daddy," she said, hesitating with well-warranted caution. "Daddy?"

Our father tore himself away from our mother's tears to look at his younger daughter. "You're here. Oh, my, how you've grown. Lissie, come here."

He swallowed her in a fatherly embrace and kissed her cheeks and forehead. "My little one," he said. "It is so good to see you. You look healthy. I've missed you so much."

He hugged her again, gripping her so tightly I could see her start to cringe.

"Daddy," she said, pulling away. "Mommy and you need to eat a fruit. It will help you feel better."

"A fruit? Oh, you're pretending, aren't you? Are you Mother Nature, all wreathed in vines and leaves?" He laughed, then reached over to include Mom, bringing her hand into his lap.

Mrs. Turner

They had told me that he wouldn't understand. They were right. Lissie wasn't wearing clothes, not because she was pretending, but because she'd turned into a wild thing without proper supervision. But how did I tell Gary that? I dried up my tears and tried to calm myself. My husband needed me.

I reached out for a fruit and took it, then bit into it. "The Gorla fruit is delicious, honey. I ate one yesterday. Try one."

He looked up at me and shook his head. "You know there's no nutrition in that, dear. You need some real food. I'll take you to the ship's canteen. Their food is pretty okay." He started to rise from the chair, then stopped. "Wait a minute. How did you get up on the ship?"

Danuel

Lissie, apparently getting tired of all this slow-motion acclimation, blurted out. "You're on the ground, Dad. Geez, and you gotta eat the fruit so you get better."

"Lissie," both of them called out in an irritated tone that meant they didn't like her giving them orders. Strange, before they would have thought she was cute. I wondered why that no longer applied. During my visits delivering groceries, I'd watched them allow Lissie to get away with all kinds of nonsense prior to Mr. Turner's departure into space.

"Just eat it," Lissie ordered brusquely, practically shoving the fruit at her father.

Lissie's mother grabbed the fruit and then tried to hand it to him. "The canteen's not open," she told him. "You'd better just eat this. It will tide you over."

"That attitude is not appropriate, young lady," he told Lissie. "I think someone needs to be sent to her room or spanked."

Koosk looked worried. I could tell by the way his pedipalps were writhing. They were usually still, but at the moment, he was creating stridulation vibrations by rubbing them together, making a kind of tsch-tsch sound. If Lissie's dad didn't calm down, I suspected that Koosk might even hiss at him, the only warning the man would get before the massive spider ran forward and grabbed Lissie out of his reach or bit him.

"Caralee, let me take Miguel," I whispered. "I think . . ."

But it was too late. Koosk shot forward, hissing like a video Halloween cat. Instead of grabbing Miguel, I launched myself after the herd spider. However, how I thought I could hold back an angry Koosk was beyond comprehension.

Lissie, hearing Koosk's hiss, turned around. "Stop," she ordered. "I'm fine, Koosk."

But now there were two more characters mixed in with this mess of a reunion. I thought about retreating, but Koosk was still stridulating his palps. Mr. Turner might still be in trouble, but from his expression, he didn't seem to know that.

"What in *beans* is that thing?" he asked.

It seemed like we were now entering a loop from our first post-alien meeting. I hung back a fraction so I didn't draw his attention. I don't think he'd noticed me yet. Thankfully.

"Lissie, get away from that freak," her father said.

Oh, no. Wrong thing to say. Lissie wheeled about and glared at her father. "Don't you say mean stuff like that! I'll sic Dokófray on you, and he'll put you back to sleep."

Mrs. Turner was doing her best to soothe her husband, cooing to him like he was a baby, but it wasn't changing the hardness in his eyes. He was fully rooted in rage again, one step from Dokófray interference, just like Lissie had warned, although her words had been more in the nature of ordering an attack dog to confront a burglar. I doubted Dokófray would appreciate that.

Obviously, Dokófray didn't. "Koosk, remove the child," the alien ordered as he walked into sight of the newly awakened couple.

"Who or what are you?" the father demanded.

"He's my friend," Lissie said just before Koosk seized her in his arms and carted her away. She wasn't happy about that. We could hear her yelling as Koosk carried her off at full gallop.

"Lissie!" Mr. Turner sprang up from the chair and tried to give chase. That lasted for two steps before he collapsed. This time, I didn't get to him in time, but his wife was there to hold him in her arms afterward. "It's okay, sweetie," she was telling him. "Koosk is her pet. He won't hurt her."

At least she remembered that. Maybe the fruits were finally getting into her system.

Caralee shoved Miguel into my arms and ran to her father. "Daddy, are you alright?" she cried out.

"Caralee!" He was a happy parent suddenly. He forgot about the alien and some giant herd spider stealing away his younger daughter. He hugged and kissed his older daughter.

"Who is this beautiful young woman? I left a child, and here we have an almost grown woman."

He kissed her again, then looked at his wife. "Why didn't you tell me the girls were here?"

"I forgot," she said in a small, unsure voice. "How could I have forgotten?"

"It doesn't matter, Mom," Caralee assured her. "It's okay. We're all going to be fine. We just have to . . ."

"Why are you dressed like Lissie? Didn't your mother have the money for clothes?" Dad said, trying to make light of it, but his eyes had found the alien, and his nose was wrinkled in bewilderment like he suddenly remembered how it was Dokófray who had ordered Lissie removed.

"Am I dreaming all this? I wanted so long to see you all, and now you're here where you couldn't possibly be."

"It does seem like a dream. I've thought that, too," Mrs. Turner said.

The two were again staring eye-to-eye, their hands entwined, but the moment before of happiness looked shadowed by their current incomprehension. Their faces showed frowns and wrinkled puzzlement. They knew something was wrong, but not what.

"Let's get you two back in your chairs," Caralee said.

I wanted to dash in and help them, especially Mr. Turner, who couldn't seem to get up on his own, but Caralee and her mother seemed up to the task, and I had Miguel in my arms. I looked down at the baby and saw that he was fully awake and watching everything. How long had he been observing? Did he realize these were his grandparents? What was I thinking? Of course, he didn't. He was only a baby. Most of the time.

Caralee deserved a top rating as a mediator. She kidded and teased her father into eating the fruit. Then she introduced Dokófray without a word about his being an alien or having conquered the planet. I think her father believed that Dokófray was just another big herd spider, one who talked.

Then, my sweet wife went on to admit that she was having trouble with Lessie and was so glad that they were ready to take back the reins because she said that she was failing miserably at being a good parent to her sister. "I think that's why she came across as such a brat. She's been missing you so much and is all confused inside."

Caralee's mother's forehead slightly puckered at that. "It hasn't been that long," she said. "I was home with you girls just a day ago. I think." Then she looked around and sat back in her chair, trying to riddle that out. Perhaps she was thinking about how much older her daughters looked. Maybe she was even remembering the place she'd awakened and how overgrown it had looked.

"No matter. You did the best you could, Caralee. We're proud of you. Lissie has always been difficult. We'll sort it out," her father said.

More hugs and kisses then, and the three were smiling. I wondered when I'd get reinserted into the equation, but I had lots of time to wait for an introduction. Already, this was going better than the first time.

"Introduce your husband, Caralee," Dokófray said.

Like a rock flying into a window, everything shattered. Darn him.

Chapter Four

Dokófray

Kids do a good job. Then orders come. Turndaloff delivers directives. *Get the two newly awakened adults, First Father, First Mother, and Spider King off the ship.*

Turndaloff hints contamination. Ship plastic. Burska impatient. Want action? Momentum accelerate.

"Introduce husband, Caralee."

Danuel with Miguel. Baby awake. Miguel eager for contact. Baby cognizant. Miguel know what Burska know. He provides eyes and ears. He tells all.

Danuel walk forward. He know consequence. I will not allow reprimand of First Father. No more.

"What does the herd spider mean that Danuel's your husband?" Caralee's father yelled.

Caralee starts explanation. I move close. "Enough. Coddling inefficient. You repeat. They forget. No more."

I meet an awakened gaze. Use full amplitude. "You listen. You learn. I tell Danuel marry. I tell Caralee marry. They make Miguel. Grandson now. Be happy or sleep."

"Sleep?" the male echoed.

"Leave ship. Burska say." I turn to Danuel. "We . . ."

"Hold it. We can't leave the ship. We're in space, you crazy spider. Why is anyone listening to this . . . this thing?"

Instability present. I call Burskans to defend. They wait in ship. Wait for call.

We hear thunder approach. Artificial floor. They gallop into chamber. Five big Burskans, big like Koosk. Almost.

"Males!" The man cries out. "With venom and claws," he shouts.

Fear arches back. Stiff in awareness. Good. Fear. He listens.

"Not space. On ground. Leave now."

Caralee and women help male rise. Cannot walk.

"Burskan carry," I tell Caralee.

She nods and backs. Pulls mother to side. Whispers words. Fury comes. Man yells. Burskan arms wrap. Time urgent. Flee ship.

Danuel

So I got a reprieve. A temporary reprieve on a loop of repetition. I laughed inwardly, then shrugged. Miguel looked up at me and grinned. The fact that we were clomping along on a big herd spider was such a fact of his existence that he didn't seem to notice that we were passing trees and in new territory where he hadn't been before. Where were we headed?

"Fa fa," Miguel proclaimed.

My smile widened, but I tried to correct him. "Da da, daddy,"

He shook his head. "Fa fa."

Okay, it could be worse. He could call me poop head like my pal, Rizzo, called his old man. That, Rizzo told me, was a joke from when he was little. Not my kind of joke.

I wondered if Rizzo was in stasis. Or was he one of the kids sent into the woods, the ones that failed? He was listed with a mate, JoJo. Not a bad-looking girl. Rizzo said he was lucky. But she wasn't all that smart. I'd had some classes with her. She said one time that we brought the herd of spiders with us from Earth. Duh.

I'd asked her if she knew how big Earth spiders were. When she shook her head, I showed her with my fingers. "Most of them measure only an inch. The biggest is a foot long."

"Oh," she said. "They sure got big when they came here."

Rizzo and JoJo in the woods? I couldn't even imagine it. Rizzo was lazy. He would have . . . well, never tried to build a hut, for one thing, and JoJo would have refused to get her fingernails dirty. Would living off the land have worked for them? Would they have survived? What did Dokófray say had happened to the failures, the ones who hadn't made it? Stasis or . . . Another question to ask him. But answers were never a surety. Or rather, it was more of a certainty that he wouldn't answer anything.

Miguel was studying my face. I looked down at him and suddenly remembered how he could mind link. Was he following my thoughts about JoJo and Rizzo and, worse, about Dokófray? What could I do to keep Miguel out of my thoughts? What happened when my thoughts were even worse than those about Rizzo and JoJo? What about when Caralee and I were thinking about the things we did in bed?

Four score and seven years ago, our fathers . . . I started reciting, hoping that would clean out my brain cells.

Miguel began to giggle. He flashed a picture of me presenting that in speech class. There I was, knees knocking, pale as school paste, and a swelling pimple on my face, right on my chin, a big beacon of red.

"Okay," I said, "Laugh, but you can't be dipping in my mind just any time. Daddies need privacy.

"Who are you talking to?" Caralee asked, butting her hips against mine even while she was riding a spider. I had no idea how she could manage to get her spider that close. But the important thing was that her parents were only a couple of herd spiders away. His father was probably steaming right now.

"Miguel," I answered. "He was making fun of me that day in speech class. I had a big red pimple on my chin and had to stand up in front of the class to recite the Gettysburg address."

Caralee held out her hands to take the baby from me. She didn't seem all that alarmed by the pimple on my face back then or the fact that our baby had the ability to make fun of his daddy.

"You're so ridiculous," she said as she bared her breast slightly to nurse Miguel. "I bet no one noticed."

"Yeah, they did. Matteo snickered over it, and Carolina commented that she could hardly concentrate on the speech because she was trying not to look at the gross thing on my chin."

"I didn't know her. I knew who Matteo was, though. He used to sing in the choir whenever my parents took me to concerts."

"Should I be jealous?"

"Fat chance. Don't you know that you were the handsomest guy there? All the girls thought so."

"And did my wife?"

"Yes, but after they listed me, I was too scared to look at you anymore."

"So you used to look at me?"

"No. Never," she said, but I could tell she way lying. For one thing, I now had some kind of lie detector planted in my brain that registered anyone's deceit, but even more simple than that, I could feel Caralee's emotions. Whenever she attempted a fib, her guilt over doing so flashed like a neon sign on an old Earth video.

I looked down at the baby, still at Caralee's breast. He was finished, just blowing milk bubbles, after having sampled both breasts. He was watching us with that smile on his face that looked like he was privy to even more than we were saying.

I wondered if Caralee knew that we should be careful what we were thinking about. I started to tell her my worries when Lissie rode up on Koosk.

"Tell me what happened," she said.

Mrs. Turner

This was all so strange. Gary said his ship was never supposed to have landed. He was very upset about that and wanted to know where the captain was. He kept spouting out, well, nonsense, about how we should be fighting the spiders, especially that Dok spider.

I had a vague memory of being told that Dokófray was not a herd spider but an alien. Carolee had said that he was the one in charge. I'd heard her tell Lissie the night before that Dokófray had gone back to his spaceship to sleep. But I didn't want to tell Gary these things. He was already upset about his grounded space ship and the way they'd carried him off it against his will. To leave the ship without the captain's permission was a court martial offense, he kept saying.

I wish he'd forget that and concentrate on the girls. I was worried about them. Caralee was nursing a baby. She was too young to have a baby. I remembered that Dokófray said he forced Danuel and her together, but was she happy? Was Danuel good to her?

And poor Lissie was carried away by that giant beast. Was she okay?

While Gary and I had been working, something horrible had happened in Beutnik. I wasn't sure what, but I thought that the five of us might be the only humans left. Where was everyone else? Were they like Gary when I'd first seen him? *Stasis*, Caralee had called it.

"Jana, are you listening?" my husband wanted to know.

I nodded, mainly just to reassure him, but I was feeling very uneasy about everything. For one thing, where were the doctors and my patients? I had work to do. I needed to get back to the hospital. I called out for Caralee, but she didn't seem to hear me. Where was that Dokófray alien? I called his name, too, making Gary very unhappy. But Dokófray didn't ride over to me either. If I knew how to steer the beast I was on, I'd direct him back to the hospital. That would be the right thing to do.

"Hospital, hospital," I yelled several times, but the spider I was on kept plodding along. Only Gary next to me seemed to hear me, and he was back to worrying about being court marshaled.

Danuel

We bedded down that night near some tree-laden fruit. One of the younger spiders again brought additional fruits for the girls' parents. I held onto Miguel and stayed away from them, letting Caralee soothe their needs.

When my wife returned, she was fretting about it. Neither of her parents seemed totally sane, she said. They'd forgotten most of what we'd told them again, so Dokófray had been right. Caralee said her dad complained about being hungry, but he'd already eaten two fruits. Mom said she would love a veg burger. She never ate veg burgers. She was a salad person.

Caralee cried a bit, then kissed the baby and tucked herself into my embrace. I pulled a blanket over us, more for privacy than warmth, since the fruits always kept us at a perfect temperature. We closed our eyes and were half asleep when the Turners started yelling. The mother kept wanting to go back to the hospital, although we'd told her that nobody was there. The father wanted to return to his ship. It was half an hour before a male herd of spiders finally gave up and bit each of them. Then, the night was blessedly quiet, and we closed our eyes and slept.

In the morning, we were right back up on the spiders, marching wherever Dokófray and Burska had decided to take us. It seemed odd to me that with Dokófray's technology, he didn't just haze us there. If he could lift us through the atmosphere and up into his ship, couldn't he transport us to our destination? But who could ever understand the aliens' thoughts? Maybe Koosk? Or maybe my son, but he was too sleepy-eyed to plant any pictures in my mind.

We passed through woods that were dark and further on, woods with flowers and sunshine. Finally, when we were ready to stop for the night, we realized that we'd returned to our home by the raging river. It felt like a great weight sliding off my back. There was our shabby looking hut, still standing, and the place we liked to sit and eat our fruit.

Over there was the sitting place, the log that wasn't all that comfortable, next to the boulder that was even less so. Down there was the beach where Lissie liked to make her sandcastles. I felt like whooping and hollering, except herd spiders don't like loud noises, so I kept my glee inside. Anyway, I guess after a trip, it always feels great to finally return home.

As darkness fell around us, Caralee and I headed inside our hut. Neither of us took the time to situate her parents. We were just too exhausted to deal with them. I suppose they were surrounded by herd spiders. I knew Lissie wasn't catering to them either because by the time Caralee and I had finished our personal needs and fed Miguel, Lissie was already curled up asleep in the hut, wrapped up in Koosk's many spider legs.

The night was short. Morning came early. The sky was still a haze of gray when I heard Mr. Turner yelling. He was going on and on about court martials and said that the military police were going to throw him in the brig if he didn't return at once. Caralee only groaned and turned over. She was sleep-breathing when I next looked. Miguel was awake, though, so my night of sleep was over. I got up, chewed some gorla fruit and fed a mouthful of the chewed gorla. Miguel was very content with that and smiled up at me, saying, "Fa fa" again.

I was too tired to teach him Da da. I just let it go.

So Caralee was sleeping, Lissie and Koosk were snoring away, and Miguel was bright-eyed and ready for adventure. What's a daddy to do but be the entertainment? I grabbed a blanket in case Miguel got cold, although I'd never seen him shiver or act the least bit chilled. Perhaps the milk he got from Caralee provided the same warming benefits as our daily dose of fruit.

A little light was being cast off by Mr. Swagman, Beatnik's biggest moon. I mean, Burska's biggest moon. I wondered if she had names for her four moons as we did: Mr. Swagman, Lord Tramp, Lady Hobo, and Sir Vagabond. Dokófray had never ordered us to call them by new names as he had the planet. Maybe the moons weren't sapient.

Someone had brought fresh fruits and laid them at the eating site. I picked up one and nibbled, giving Miguel pasty bites when he indicated he wanted them with an open mouth of eagerness, but he wasn't really hungry anymore. He was more interested in looking around, which he did with the constant movement of his head and eyes.

A large female herd spider moved closer to Miguel and me. She bowed her head and sat down closer than I might have wanted, but after we sat there a minute or two, I realized it was actually nice to have her company. I placed Miguel down in the dirt, and, of course, he crawled directly to her. I figured that was probably what both of them wanted anyway. I was certainly not the main attraction.

Miguel climbed her legs, then almost pulled himself higher before his lack of stability started to cause him to fall. No worries, of course. The spider wrapped its legs around him and protectively anchored him exactly where he wanted to be. The goo goo gaa gaa's flowed, and the baby talk that he liked to chant rose up in song. Before I knew it, he was singing to a whole group of spiders, all gathered around us, adoring him.

"What is that horrid noise?" came the ugly shout of Caralee's father.

Speaking of ugly noises, I thought, but I didn't say anything. His wife accompanied him over to our private space. Her eyes fastened on the baby surrounded as he was by hairy spider legs.

She suddenly stopped, froze, and then screamed.

Caralee came running out of the hut, followed by Koosk and Lissie. But nothing was wrong with her mother. She was just standing there screaming as if the world were ending.

Miguel turned to look at her. His head tilted, and he stared. Then he saw his mother. "Ma ma," he screeched.

Our home used to be a quiet place, I thought to myself, but if the girls were happier with their parents here, I knew I'd have to get used to a lot of drama and screams.

Caralee walked over to the baby and swept him up. Then she thanked the female spider for watching him. What was I, invisible?

Caralee shot a giggle my way, obviously picking up my thought, and then she headed toward me and sank into my open-wide arms.

"Never invisible, my husband," she said as she kissed my lips with a good morning kiss.

At some point, Mrs. Turner had stopped screaming and was standing there merely watching. She sank down in the dirt so gracefully it was like she planned it, but I think the shock had hit her and collapse just seemed the easiest thing to do.

Miguel couldn't be hungry, having eaten quite a bit of the gorla fruit, but he squawked until Caralee attached him to a breast. Then he drank at the most a minute and stopped to turn his head so he could watch both people and spiders. Both seemed to fascinate him more than his mother's milk at that moment.

"Weren't you afraid they might hurt the baby?" Mrs. Turner finally asked when she was no longer hyperventilating.

"No. They love Miguel. He's their Spider Hopper."

"What does that mean?"

Caralee shrugged. "I have absolutely no idea. I've asked and asked, but no one will tell me."

"I know," Lissie said. "He's Burska's Spider King."

"And what does that mean?" we all wanted to know, but Lissie either didn't know or didn't want to tell us. She skipped away, heading for the beach and her sandcastles.

"Don't go too far," her mother said, but Lissie didn't pay her the slightest bit of attention.

Mrs. Turner watched as Koosk followed after her. "He won't hurt her, right?" she asked.

Caralee had her mouth full of Gola fruit. She shook her head and indicated that her mom should eat one of the fruits.

"They're not nutritious for us," Caralee's father said, but he grabbed up two, then handed one to his wife. Sitting beside her, they both ate their fruits without further argument.

It was a very strange day. The herd of spiders stayed close. Lissie did her thing with the sandcastles, and Caralee and I sewed on the hats we'd decided to make. Her father seemed mellower and was interested in what we were doing, but he scoffed over our desire to make Burska clothes.

"We have tons of clothes back in the city. Caralee. I bet you still have clothes at the house. Why aren't you living there? Why go primitive?"

She didn't have to answer. Dokófray had dropped in.

Dokófray

"You do not change this. Burska demands."

"Yeah, well, I don't follow that religion. Burska? You mean Beatnik?" Without waiting for an answer, Mr. Turner continued talking. "Beatnik is just a planet. It doesn't get to tell us what to do. The kids fell for that malarkey, but I'm not going to. There is absolutely no reason . . ."

"First Father, First Mother desire you awakened," I tell the father of Caralee and Lissie. "But I think, undesirable. Opinionable. Unstable. Better not awakened."

I look at Danuel. His face is not happy. He frowns like Lissie. Like Caralee. No happiness for waking up these people.

I shake my head. I know what happen soon. They will not like it. Lissie will not like it. The whole ship not like.

But Burska say make effort. Train. We feed fruit. Feed new fruit. No change.

"Danuel, Caralee. Talk sense or . . ." I say.

I visit Lissie. She plays in sand. She delights us. We like. But she goes. Soon. Many go. Great sadness. Necessary.

Chapter Five

Caralee

Dokófray must think Danuel and I are miracle workers. How are we supposed to talk Dad into anything? He's stubborn. I never realized it before. Was it being on that ship for so long, or has he always been like this? I would ask Mom, but she's still in her mental fog, dangling between the old memories and the new. The fruit doesn't seem to be helping. Maybe Miguel is the secret. He is her grandson. She has to learn to care for him, doesn't she?

Right now, Mom is all concerned about Dad, who's frozen again. Dokófray put him back into stasis. Or so we thought.

Lissie later left the sand to tell us that we should talk to Dad as if he were awake. She says he will slowly waken then. He is not in stasis, only in a deep sleep state. But isn't that what stasis is?

I wanted to see my parents, but this isn't going well. Poor Danuel never knows when one of my parents will start lashing out at him again and call him a pedophile. It was never like that. He tried so hard to wait. Sometimes, I envy Lissie, who is able to leave all the stress behind and get consumed in fantasy sandcastles and river dragons. Only I wouldn't give up Miguel and Danuel for anything, so there is that.

Miguel is awake. He's staring at Danuel and Dad. He has started singing again. Usually, when he does that, the spiders crawl closer and then crowd around him, but instead, like Miguel, they're watching Dad. But Dad's not moving. He's frozen exactly how Dokófray left him, so what is there to look at? The spiders observed lots of people stiff as posts at the ship and in *Stasis Village*, which is what Danuel and I have dubbed the little shacks where all the city people are standing, horizontally stacked.

Danuel is standing next to Dad, not poking him (or slugging him, which I felt he wanted to do at times) but talking to him. I wonder what he's saying. Just like that, with my curiosity stabbed, the mental link opened up, and I could hear Danuel's words.

"The hut is lopsided. I want to improve it, but I have no idea what to do. I thought maybe you might have some thoughts. Did you ever build a treehouse on Earth? I've seen pictures of them. Or a clubhouse, like some kids had. Anything you can suggest would be appreciated.

"I know you don't see eye-to-eye with me, but it's for your daughters and your grandson. When the rains come, we need a leakproof shelter. I'm using turtle shells now, but the reeds keep allowing them to shift in the downpours. Then I have to go out and reformat them while the rain puddles into our hut.

"There's no disease for us. Dokófray says we're immune to everything, but it can't be healthy for a baby to be constantly getting wet, and Lissie, too. She's four now, but that's still in the baby category, I figure. I have to keep her dry. And Caralee, of course. I love your daughter, Sir, and I want to build something that makes her feel safe and secure. Will you help me?'

"Dokófray said you'd be coming out of this deep sleep bit soon. Although we never know exactly what he means by soon. Sometimes, that's the next day, and other times it's weeks away. But anyway, if you don't do as he orders, or even if you say things he doesn't like, he'll come do this again. He could leave you in stasis forever, and then Caralee and Lissie would be left to view you as nothing more than a statue. You don't want that, do you?

"You see, we really don't have a choice in what we do. The planet and the aliens — you've seen only one alien, but there are others up on that ship. They kind of tortured us up there for a while. Well, maybe not tortured exactly, but no toilet, no food, and no water for several days. We had to accept their lessons, and we learned that bucking them amounted to penalties and unpredictable punishments.

"At first, Lissie, Caralee, and I were in separate rooms. That was a bargaining point. But then they put us together. Lissie kept causing trouble. She did the banana thing, but Dokófray wouldn't give her any fruit until she buckled down. She still doesn't obey him that much, but Koosk protects her. He's always stealing her away when punishment is pending, like when Lissie kicked Dokófray because he put you back into stasis.

"You need to know that I took care of the girls for a long time before Dokófray married Caralee and me. I love your daughter, but I never would have . . . well, that's Burska, the planet's design. She wanted Miguel. We don't understand about that part. About the spider hopping. No one ever explains things with any clarity. They just leave us wallowing in doubt and confusion. You get used to that. Ask a question, and they walk away.

"Lissie gets more out of Dokófray than the rest of us. He really likes her. At least, I think so since she seems to get special treatment. Maybe that's why Koosk adopted her.

"You have to understand, Sir, that we tried to go back to the farm. Caralee wanted those clothes you were talking about. We tried to return there. We captured herd spiders and rode them to the orchard, but Dokófray wouldn't allow Caralee to go home. He put up a wall. Caralee cried a lot over that. We're pretty much just winging it here. We have to make do with what they give us or what we can find and figure out.

"Sorry, I guess I've done a lot of babbling. I don't know what else to say. We want to wake up more of the people, but I think Dokófray is waiting to see if you calm down and become agreeable to meeting Burska's demands. That means living off the land. No artificial things like plastic. No food that's not from Burska's trees. Dokófray told us once that Burska would provide almost anything we needed. We keep forgetting to ask about apples and bananas. I don't know if she can grow those, but Dokófray said she probably could.

"It would be great if you guys would help us instead of fighting us. Otherwise, I'm afraid of what Burska and Dokófray will do. They probably won't kill anyone, but they might decide to keep everyone in stasis. Please don't make them do that. Caralee and Lissie deserve to have their parents back. But that's up to you.

"Miguel is your grandson. I hope you accept him as yours. He's a fine baby. Caralee and I love him very much. But he can do things we don't understand. He talks to the planet, for one thing. And for another, you know that noise you complained about, well, that was the baby singing. The song attracts the herd of spiders. They gather around him to listen. I don't understand the message, but I think there must be something there. Or else they just like to hear him singing. I could use your help figuring all that out.

"Anyway, that's all I have to say. Oh, except if you eat the native fruit, it might help you. That's what made Caralee and me immune to diseases. "

Caralee

When Danuel came back, I gave him the biggest hug and kiss ever. It made Miguel really laugh. His song stopped, and he sent an image. Baby Alexandro. It was the blond-haired toddler Danuel had seen. I wondered if that meant I was pregnant again, but Miguel shook his head. Should babies do that? Of course, to classify Miguel with other babies was hardly fair. He was the Spider Hopper.

Miguel laughed at that thought, his mouth open, displaying zero teeth. When did babies grow in their teeth? I wanted to ask Mom, but she'd been dicey since Dad's exit into Zombieville.

I decided to copy what Danuel had done. I sat down near my mother and began to talk to her. I told her how I'd like to get her help in raising Miguel. I didn't have the education she did, and I needed her to teach Miguel about Earth and nursing and all the things I'd missed by not finishing school. I told her that I really didn't know how to be a mother. I needed her.

But like Dad, she didn't speak, didn't even look at me. I didn't know if she could hear me. I had no idea if my words were getting inside her.

"I never learned to cook," I told her. "Or sew. Could you teach me how to work with spider silk? I knew some people had made beautiful sweaters from the web silk. Do you think the silk could be colored with fruits?" I asked.

"Fruits and nuts," she said. "Maybe even soaking twigs or leaves."

"Mom, you're awake," I said, my voice rising in pitch with my excitement.

Miguel stopped singing to look at me. Then his big toothless grin widened as he turned his head to see his grandmother.

She held out her arms. "May I hold him, please?"

All right, a moment's trepidation, but it was my mother. I passed Miguel into her arms and moved closer, just in case.

When my father finally came out of his somnolent state, he, too, seemed more ready to accept things as they were. Practically, the first thing he said was, "Let me see this tree house/hut you're talking about, Danuel."

When he did, he couldn't find much to praise. He moved on, asking about available resources, and Danuel and he strode off into the woods to investigate. On the way, Danuel said they discussed how the aliens had invaded and what the city people had done about that. Danuel couldn't tell him anything about what happened there, just what we'd seen and done when their ships landed.

"What were you doing at the farmhouse that day?" Dad wanted to know, and Danuel explained about being there because he was delivering groceries.

I started to have hope that my parents would pull out of their stupor. On double fruits and the special one that Burska had made for them, perhaps we'd soon see some improvement. I had my fingers crossed.

Over the next few days, things progressed well. My parents stopped berating Danuel, Lissie came and sat on her father's lap, and Dad learned not to say bad things about Koosk. I thought things were going well.

Only Dad got it in his mind that the only way to make a solid house was for us to cut down some trees. Danuel and I weren't sure if Burska would approve. It was a question for Dokófray since we didn't have a direct line to Burska. Of course, Miguel might have given us advice, too, but he was busy playing the baby with his grandparents and the strange singing and communing seemed to have departed temporarily.

When our mental communications with Dokófray went ignored, we asked Lissie, but she was too busy making moats and castles for the sea creatures down in the sandy area where she liked to play. Dad tried to pull her away by scolding her. That was the worst thing he could do. She and Koosk disappeared for the better part of a day.

Dad said that we didn't need to ask permission because we'd be doing exactly what Burska wanted us to do, which was to live off the land. Maybe he was right, but when Danuel and I discussed it, we had a bad feeling about it. Chopping down her trees didn't seem to be something she'd approve of.

But Dad took things in his own hands. When we woke up one morning, he was gone. Several hours later, he appeared, dragging a huge tree trunk. He was red in the face and panting hard. We all worried about him and got him to drink some water and eat a Gorla fruit. He looked better after that. But then we found out that he'd used a metal knife to make his axe. Not a good thing. Burska would not appreciate that.

But nothing happened. The days went by, Dad and Danuel continued their building project, and Mother started teaching me first aid. Danuel probably could have taught me the same thing, but it was nice for both Mom and me to work together on something. We spent our day trading stories as well as taking care of Miguel.

But neither the flow of a river nor human life runs smoothly. I woke up one morning sick. The remnants of my dinner the night before, plus half of my stomach lining, poured into a turtle shell that Danuel had handed me. When I lay back on the bed, emptied, Danuel asked me if he should hunt for some Chuga root. That's when it hit me. Pregnant.

I closed my eyes and thought of the little blonde boy we'd watched in the image Miguel had sent. The toddler had been playing with a herd spider. Was this our Alexandro?

It was Dad who interrupted us. "Hey, sleepy heads," he said, invading our space. "Aren't you two getting up this morning?"

"We can't tell him," I said, worried because things had been improving, and this would probably be a big setback.

Danuel nodded. I think he was relieved.

Lissie

Something bad was coming. I couldn't tell what, and Koosk wasn't answering my questions. In fact, he'd been acting strange. It was like he didn't want to tell me something and was putting if off.

I pleaded and scratched all the places he liked me to scratch, but his eyes peered into the distance, and he acted like I wasn't as important to him as I used to be.

I talked to Danuel about it. He tilted his head and looked over at Koosk. "Maybe he has a girlfriend."

That was a really nasty thought. I didn't want Koosk having girlfriends or even close friends among the herd spiders. He was my best friend. He didn't need anyone else.

"What if Miguel were older and wanted to do things with you?" Danuel asked. "Wouldn't he become your closest buddy then?"

"Would he dig in the sand with me and make castles?"

Danuel shrugged. "Ask him. He might communicate with you."

I didn't know what that word meant, but Danuel explained that Miguel might send me pictures. That sounded like fun.

I went running over to the baby, but he was asleep. I wanted to wake him up, but my real mom was holding him, and she said no. 'When will he wake up?"

Mommy and Caralee had been spending a lot of time together, but I hadn't. My real mommy didn't like the sand, and she never wanted to swim. She really didn't do much except talk with Dad, Danuel, and my sister. But talking was boring. I wanted to go places and do things.

Daddy was trying to be nicer now about Koosk, but Daddy still said things he shouldn't, like about Dokófray. Sometimes, I had to stop him from saying mean things. He didn't like that, but Mommy and Daddy had calmed down. They didn't yell anymore. I think because of the fruit. They were eating a lot of it. Daddy was helping Danuel, too. That was nice. Our new hut was going to be bigger, Danuel said.

Daddy started telling me a story about exploring planets. I liked hearing about that. I wanted to know if other planets had herd spiders, but he said no. I didn't want to live on a planet that didn't have aliens or herd spiders. Daddy said that we might have to if Burska said to. But why would Burska say that? She liked us. We were hers. Koosk had told me that.

But grownups always said things like that. They always wanted to think of bad things.

Daddy told me about his favorite planet where there were giant butterflies. He said they were red and orange or blue and yellow. The butterflies landed on people, but they didn't bite or anything. They just sat there flapping their wings. Then they flew away. That sounded nice. I wanted to see giant butterflies. Daddy said there were other animals on the planet. Some were bad animals. They wanted to eat us. So, I guess I won't go see the giant butterflies. I don't want to get eaten.

Daddy said that Earth might pay us a lot of money to help the people settle there. He said Mommy, and he were thinking about going. Then, we could all live like we wanted without a planet telling us what to do. I didn't like that. I told Daddy that I would never leave Koosk and Burska. Burska was my home.

Daddy's face got red. He looked like he was getting angry again, so I stood up and was just about to go back to the sand when Miguel looked at me; he opened his mouth to cry about wanting milk.

"No, Miguel," I said. "I wanna talk to you."

Mommy started explaining how babies couldn't talk, but I ignored her. I knew about Miguel communicating. Danuel had said so.

Miguel closed his mouth and stared into my eyes. He got really serious then. I didn't want Mommy and Daddy to hear me, so I sent questions in my head. *Will you play in the sand with me soon? Do you like to build castles?*

Miguel blinked, then yawned. He did big yawns. Really wide and full. But his mouth was still empty. No tooths yet, so it was a big pink gummy mouth of a yawn.

He nodded his head. Then he sent me a picture. He was laughing in the picture, and we were digging in the sand. He was leaning on my shoulder, but then he tumbled over. I helped him stand back up, but there was sand all over him, so I wiped it off his body. Again, he grinned, but I was surprised to see that in the picture, he had two tooths on the bottom of his gums and two tooths on the top.

He giggled. He thought that was very funny. I showed him my tooths. I had a lot of them. He reached out and touched my tooths, then poked a finger at his gums like he was checking for tooths in his mouth.

Daddy tried to interrupt us. I shushed him. I wanted to talk more with Miguel, but I guess he was done talking. He looked at Grandpa, then at his grandma, and smiled.

They cooed over Miguel, telling him what a good baby he was. I guess they weren't angry about him being part of our family anymore. I hoped that was how they'd feel about the new baby who was coming. But Koosk had told me not to tell, so I didn't.

I went back to the sand, feeling better. Miguel wanted to play in the sand with me. Soon. So if Koosk was gone, it was ok. I guess Koosk needed a girlfriend. I remembered how Danuel used to look love sick all the time when Caralee didn't want him around. She was kind of mean to him. He was always doing nice things, too. I guessed boys needed girlfriends. But why wouldn't Koosk tell me?

Dokófray

Gary Turner is not adapting. Wife is better, but Burska say fruits not make healthy. They calm, but fruit not help body. Too bad. Caralee very happy. Danuel, too.

Burska say Gary and Jana talk about leave. They go Butterfly Planet. On ship we discuss this. We know Little Lissie must go. She belong with parents. Not stay with Danuel, Caralee, Miguel. Too bad.

Koosk knows. He wants tell Lissie. Burska say no.

Children need more time with Jana, Gary. But we do what Burska say.

Do we wake more people?

Burska say not yet. She feels happy. Baby two comes. Miguel strong, healthy. Perhaps we wake only young? Burska still say no. Give more time. Fix house. Tree loss not good. But maybe necessary. She thinks on that.

She say need more fruits. More roots. She works on that. Variety is good for children. More people mean more trees. Busy Burska. I ask bananas and apples. She laughs. The planet laughs but not many times. She say she grow bananas and apples for Lissie.

I say Linnie not want to go. She want stay with Koosk.

Yes, Burska say. But no. She go with parents. She has purpose. Is needed. She return someday. She come back. I smile then. I smile big.

Gary Turner

Okay. I get it. The alien tells Caralee and Danuel what to do. They accept it. They should not. I will have to convince them to come with us. When they hear that we plan to go, they will surely be willing.

All last night, Jana and I whispered, discussing the Butterfly Planet. There is danger on that planet, but we can hunt for meat. We can eat the plants and drink the water. With guns, we can defend ourselves. It is like it was on early Earth when predators still roamed. But it's exciting to think about. A new planet to civilize, and we will be in the ones in charge. Earth has promised us that. Governmental positions. The settlers will look to us since we have experience in farming and adapting to new environments. It will be a good thing.

The biggest problem will be the ship. How do we get the ship to lift up? Will the aliens help us once they learn we want to leave? If humans leave their Beatnik, Burska, that will actually solve their problems. No more humans destroying their planet. It is everything they want.

Especially when they find out that waking people up is going to provoke chaos, no one will listen to aliens telling us what to do — or some nebulous planet that supposedly talks. She hasn't talked to me. That's for sure.

I wonder how I contact that Doko guy and ask him about such things. I know that he's been silent. The kids are still worried about the tree I cut down. They fear Doko's rage. They shouldn't have to live in fear. That's ridiculous. Besides, the alien is probably making all this up. Maybe that ship up in space has a bunch of aliens laughing over the stupidity of us humans, believing this planet's sentience stuff. I bet that's it. It's a show to them. A comedy, no doubt.

Jana is worried that the kids won't go with us, but I'll just tell them that's what we're doing. They're still minors. They can't disobey. If necessary, I'll get others to round them up, but I wouldn't want to have to do that. It would be embarrassing not to have control over my own children. Perhaps I'll just steal Miguel. Then they'd have to come. Yes, that would work well.

But first, I need to talk with Doko. We need to wake up the captain and talk him into returning to Butterfly Planet. Earth can send her settlers if we offer coordinates. But it would be best to construct some dwellings first. A base for our government. I suppose the captain will be president. What position will he offer me? Vice President will do.

Jana is valuable. She is a full nurse. But we'll be waking up all the hospital staff, so . . .

Danuel

The tree stabilized the house. Mr. Turner gave me permission to call him Gary. Gary says that lumber is the cornerstone of good house building. I saw immediately that he was right, but will Burska allow it? She does want us to adapt to living in a non-plastic and nonmetal way, but she also views her fauna as an extension of herself. But since we haven't heard from Dokófray, I guess we don't need to worry about it. I think.

Caralee and her mother have been getting along well. Jana took to the baby finally, calling him *her sweet grandson*. I think that bridge has now been passed. Yesterday, I even saw Gary giving Miguel a belly tickle. Neither of them has been spouting things about returning to the ship or hospital, so I guess they finally understood that those days are gone.

I wish Lissie had shown more of an interest in getting reacquainted with her parents, but she said that every time she tried to be nice, her dad said something mean about Burska or Koosk. That was a big problem, but I told Lissie that for adults, adaptation was slow.

"Adaption?" she repeated wrongly.

"Adaptation," I said, showing her the syllables with my fingers.

"Four," she said, smiling big.

"It means it takes adults a long time to understand new things. We are slow to accept."

"Oh," she said. Dokófray said you resist change. He told me that meant you didn't want anything to change. He said you had to change, or Burska wouldn't like you anymore."

"Dokófray said that?"

Lissie had already lost interest in the subject. She was digging up some roots for our meals. I watched as she reburied the necessary piece for replanting, as Dokófray had taught us. She was an amazing four-year-old. I sometimes wondered if Dokófray knew how exceptional she was. Did her parents? Maybe that was the problem. They still thought Lissie was only a little toddler, barely able to pull up her own pants.

But Lissie was so much more. Her drawings were now recognizable. Her reading skills, thanks to Caralee's tutoring, had made it so that she could not only read a few paragraphs but write some. She probably knew about fifty words now.

I thought about the last story she wrote. Ok, it wasn't great, but for a kid her age, it was amazing:

Lissie haz a hurd spidr. She liks hur hurd spidr. She and he sleep 2gater. (together) She and he pla (play) 2gater. Lissie luvs her hurd spidr.

Full translation: *Lissie has a herd spider. She likes her herd spider. She and he sleep together. She and he play together. Lissie loves her herd spider.*

Caralee was worried about all the misspellings, but I think it's great. Now Caralee has decided their newest game will be spelling bees, so Lissie can learn to spell *spider, herd,* and *play.* I guess *together* will come next week.

Lissie's parents were happy to see her writing, too, but not as enthusiastic as they should have been. It started them worrying about Lissie not having a school to go to. But she's too young anyway.

But, just as Lissie said, we adults resist change, and for them, everything seems to set them off. They started remembering things the way they used to be before sand and sticks were a child's writing tools and how we used to have desks and school buildings.

Caralee wasn't worried. She showed them how she and Lissie were working on math problems using stones and sticks. It really is the same concept, adding and subtracting things in nature. Only they want her to have books with written number problems and calculators.

On Earth, we used to . . . became the refrain for the day. I was glad Dokófray wasn't around. He wouldn't have liked it one bit.

Chapter Six

Caralee

Mom and Dad have been with us for a while now. They are both getting thin while I'm getting fatter. The former worries me. Does that mean that they need more fruits, or are they not getting sufficient nutrition from the ones they're eating? The latter concern burdens me, too, but for a completely different reason. What will they say when they find out I'm going to have another baby?

Danuel said that it was to be expected, but this is what my parents are talking about, where one plus one does not necessarily equal two. At least not when they think I'm still too young to be married and have Miguel.

Thinking about Miguel reminds me that maybe I have a resource I'm not utilizing. I took the baby from my mom and moved down to the beach where my little sister was. She was working on a moat for her river dragons but was happy to see me. It seems that Koosk has been neglecting her lately. She sounded lonely.

Feeling a bit guilty because I never got down in the sand and played with her anymore, I sat beside her and asked if I could help. I set Miguel down beside me, and he immediately crawled over to Lissie, then hoisted himself up, leaning against her. He was giggling and started to fall, but she grabbed him and saved him from tumbling.

Miguel was so happy to be included in the activity he opened his mouth and started laughing, and Lissie cried out, "He's got teeth, Cara. Miguel has teeth!"

When I looked, I saw that she was right. How had I not known? He was still nursing me. He was still licking Gorla paste off my finger. Danuel and I should have felt the teeth.

And weren't babies going through teething supposed to cry and show the pain of teeth breaking through their gums?

Lissie got all funny about it. She told me it was the picture that Miguel had shown her a while back.

That was really eerie. Did it mean that Miguel could see into the future?

But then I remembered the picture Dokófray had shown me about Miguel being born, long before we knew there was even going to be a Miguel, and the baby had also given me a picture of Alexandro. I guessed these kinds of things were possible on Burska.

Jana Turner

Caralee came running up to share in the news. Not for the first time, I noticed that she was looking chubby around the middle. Suddenly, I knew why. My darling daughter, my very young darling daughter, was pregnant again. My heart sank.

She hadn't mentioned it to us, so I guessed she and Danuel were keeping it a secret. I knew Gary would storm. He'd lecture Caralee and rage at Danuel. But what were they supposed to do about it? There weren't any doctors out here in the wilds.

My daughter was caught up in telling me about Miguel's having teeth, four of them, she said. I knew that wasn't possible. Perhaps the baby was old enough for teeth. I had no idea how old he was, and of course, his parents didn't know. No calendars. But if Miguel had been growing teeth, he would have been feverous and fretful. Lissie cried for weeks when her first teeth were coming in. She refused to sleep. But Miguel was always smiling. I don't think I'd ever seen him sickly.

Caralee shoved him into my arms, and I saw for myself. Four teeth. There'd been no rash, no vomiting, no diarrhea, which both Lissie and Caralee had suffered through.

"Amazing," I said, shaking my head. "How could he have passed through this four times without a whimper?"

Later, when Danuel and Gary came back from their construction work, Danuel admired the teeth, but he didn't seem to understand the miracle of it. My husband remembered vividly. He'd walked many nights with Lissie in his arms, trying to soothe her teething tears.

"It was Burska's blessing," Lissie told us later when she left her sand castles to eat a fruit with us. "That's what Koosk calls things like that."

Gary snorted. "Next, you'll tell me it was those river dragons who sprinkled tooth fairy dust over the baby, or was it that herd spider of yours?"

Lissie didn't understand that he was making fun of her. But just to make sure, she came to the spider's defense. "Koosk wouldn't bite Miguel. But one of the old spiders bit Caralee. Koosk bit Danuel. The herd spiders didn't want First Mother or First Father to feel any pain. There was a lot of blood. Danuel said that was okay. But I don't think it was. It was a bad magic trick."

"A herd spider bit you?" Gary exploded. He was looking at Caralee, like the fact that a herd spider bit Danuel wasn't important.

Most of the time, my husband liked Danuel, but then, sometimes, he remembered how Danuel got Caralee pregnant when she was only fifteen. When he recalled that, he was back to storming at the boy for being irresponsible and selfish.

So the evening wasn't progressing well. Then Gary decided to tell Danuel and Caralee about his plans for Butterfly Planet. There was a full-out war following that, with everyone saying things they'd regret in the morning.

"You have to do what I tell you," Gary said, sealing off the argument as if he'd get the final word.

And then, Caralee started vomiting, and Gary stopped yelling. His face got white, and I could tell that he was already ruing the harshness of his words. But Caralee was crying by then, wanting only Danuel beside her.

"Where's that Doko guy? He needs to come and heal her right now," Gary said.

Maybe it was that plea that called the alien, or maybe it was all the screeching at each other that brought him, but whichever reason, he was suddenly there, viewing the scene with those two huge staring eyes of his and hissing up a storm at Gary.

"You take calm from First Mother? Burska is not happy. She not want you here. She says go."

I gasped, horrified to hear that. Did it mean that we would be driven away from our children? I pulled on Gary's arm, trying to get him to apologize, but he wasn't through with his avalanche of accusations.

"My daughter is sick. You need to heal her. She's only sick because you won't let her go to a doctor. She needs medication and good food. She needs to sleep in a real bed and wear clothes not tree leaves. She needs . . ."

That did it. Dokófray, as the girls had told me, was not patient. He did whatever it was to silence my husband, then turned to Caralee and Danuel.

"Get chuga root," he ordered Danuel, who nodded and went to hunt some in the hut.

"You mother of Caralee, you know she need peace, calm. She mother of Alexandro. Judge come. He healthy. But mother need rest. Not this," he said, Dokófray's top arms were waving about like a musical conductor with a fast-moving symphony.

Danuel returned with a small piece of some kind of white root we hadn't seen before. Caralee made a face, indicating that she didn't like the taste of it, but she popped it into her mouth and sucked on it. Then, sighing, she wiggled closer to Danuel the moment he sat down.

"Good," Dokófray said.

"Hut done?" the alien asked Danuel.

He nodded, but Danuel didn't look like he was quite proud of the work. "We had to kill a tree," he said, hanging his head.

"Burska knows. She permits."

Danuel let out a huge sigh of relief. I think he'd been worried about it. This relationship between the alien and the mysterious talking planet mystified me, but I didn't bring it up at that moment. Gary had done enough damage. I waited to see if the alien would remember that he'd told us to leave.

As if he heard my thought, he glanced at me. "You and Lissie father must go. Burska say. Fruit not good, not give health. You not live on planet food. You go to Butterfly. Burska say okay. She help. She lift ship."

I gasped. The alien had heard us talking in the night? What would she do? Would she punish us?

"You sleep. Tomorrow go. Koosk find spiders willing. They not like you. Difficult."

"We won't go without our children."

Danuel looked up from tending to Caralee. I could see that he was puzzled about my statement. Did he think we wouldn't take him with us?

"Yes. Lissie go. Too young. Must be with parents. We sad. But Burska say."

"Of course," I said. "We would never leave a four-year-old behind. But I mean, Caralee, Miguel, and Danuel will be going with us, too."

Danuel

Those lessons on calm deliberations that the aliens had lectured us on didn't seem to apply to Dokófray's conduct. I would call turning Jana into an unmoving column, a statue of flesh, a bad example of: *Sort differences while dialoguing.*

Dokófray glanced at both of us, then moved to Lissie. She was staring at him with an expression of stark horror.

"I won't go with them. I won't," Lissie cried out, then ran off, returning to her sand castles.

Caralee was still feeling sick. I didn't want to leave her, but it was dark out. Lissie shouldn't be alone, even if the planet lacked predators or other dangers. Accidents happened, especially when someone was upset.

"Where's Koosk?" I asked. "He's deserted Lissie of late."

Dokófray was already walking after Lissie. It looked like he would be the one to console her. He stopped and looked back. "Koosk sulks. He feels great sadness."

Dokófray took three more steps, then turned about to look over at Caralee. "Alexandro comes. Great joy. He be judge."

That was the second time Dokófray had said that about the baby being a judge. I wanted to ask what it meant, but Dokófray was suddenly gone. It was probably pointless anyway to ask him anything. The alien always left more puzzles in his wake than answers.

But Miguel was awake. He was sitting with his back against Caralee. Had he crawled there?

"Miguel is sitting up," I told my wife.

She nodded. "He is talking to me."

I went to them and sat down on the other side of Miguel. "May I tune in?" I asked.

Miguel looked up at me. He giggled, showing his new teeth. It was a surprise to see them. Had they sprouted up all at once, seemingly overnight?

The baby was projecting pictures. Caralee's parents were walking like zombies. Lissie stood between them, holding their hands. But Lissie didn't look like Lissie. Her eyes were dull. I thought that she, too, must be under alien control. We weren't there in the images. We apparently hadn't been permitted to ride to the ship with them. Just the three of them were climbing up the ship ramp and heading on inside.

Dokófray had accompanied them, but also Turndaloff and Flistercrokta waited at the side. I saw others, aliens I didn't know, although a couple looked familiar. Why had so many come? And then I remembered what Dokófray had said. They were going to lift up the ship. Was their technology that powerful?

The ship's ramp lifted, clanging closed like one of Lissie's imaginary castle draw bridges. The heavy bolt of a lock sounded. I knew then that the ship was preparing for space.

"What about the others in the city?" I asked. Miguel tilted his head and continued to stare into my eyes. I saw a line of people walking toward the ship. The ramp was still down when they arrived, so I knew this had taken place before our parents arrived. They looked drugged as well. I saw faces I recognized: the librarian, a teacher, the grocery store owner . . .

"All the people are leaving?" I asked. "Will we be the only ones left on Burska?"

Miguel shook his head, then smiled. His newly toothed gums beamed in the faint light of Mr. Swagman and Lord Tramp, the two moons currently leering down at us.

The picture rotated, and I saw the remaining pretzel people. Classmates, kids we knew, and children younger than we were by several years. None of them were Lissie's age. The youngest was maybe ten. But in the junkyard huts where we'd gone to wake Caralee and Lissie's mom, none of the sick or the adults remained. Everyone still in stasis was young.

"Birthed on Burska," I remember Lissie saying that once. She'd said it about Miguel, but it applied to most of the kids I saw in Miguel's images.

"I don't want my parents to go. Or Lissie," Caralee said.

Miguel looked sad when she said that. He turned to look at his mother. He leaned into her. His hand reached up to touch her face. The picture he showed then was of her parents getting thinner until they couldn't sit up and couldn't stand.

"Oh," Caralee said. "Burska's fruit doesn't sustain them. I understand now. But what about Lissie?"

At that moment, Lissie came walking towards us. She was crying, but not hysterically.

"Lissie need goodbye. Must go. Too young. Need parents. Burska say she teach parents, others. She come back. She visit. We bring her. But live on Butterfly," Dokófray said, his voice as sad as I'd ever heard it.

Lissie stood beside Dokófray swallowed in his leg-arms. Her head was bowed, the tears streaming down her cheeks. She ran to me. "Danuel. Caralee. I'll miss you. Dokófray says I have to go. I have to take care of my parents and the others. He says I can visit soon. What is soon, Dokófray?"

"Soon mean appropriate time."

"What about Koosk? He has a girlfriend, but he will still miss me, right?"

Dokófray sighed. Had he made that sound before he met us? None of the herd spiders ever sighed. Was that something Dokófray had picked up from us? The alien nodded his head at Lissie. "Koosk, miss you. Miguel miss you. All family miss you. We miss you."

Dokófray dropped one hairy spider arm to touch Lissie's shoulder. "Burska say she send banana and apple tree. She send in ship. Trees grow. Also, send Garla fruit, Kiginoa, and Bedorka trees. You plant. You make grow." Then, when Lissie visit, we give baby spider. You keep. Not Koosk. Too big. Too herd important. But baby, okay."

Lissie had weaned herself from her finger-sucking long ago, but all that information apparently was just too much for her. The finger jumped into her mouth, providing her a moment of comfort.

I squeezed my little sister. Danuel did, too. Then we cried. Miguel did not, but he sent a picture to Lissie. He showed a sandy area. It wasn't our beach. It looked different. Then we realized. There were butterflies. They dropped down to rest on Lissie's shoulders. They flapped their wings, and we could see she was talking to them. She looked happy.

"Will you take care of the river dragons?" Lissie asked Dokófray, but he didn't answer. When we looked up, we saw that he was gone. I'm not sure, but I might have seen tears in his eyes before he disappeared.

Koosk did not come into the hut that night to sleep with Lissie. He had been doing so less often. Breaking a rule Caralee and I had made, we invited Lissie into our bed. She nuzzled down contentedly. She snuggled up with Miguel, and then, after giving each of us a big, sloppy kiss, she fell asleep almost immediately.

Yet, in spite of sleeping between us, in the morning, we couldn't find her. She had left the hut. And when we checked in the sandy area, she was not there either, Koosk must have heard our frantic call. He suddenly appeared, and then Dokófray arrived, probably set to take Jana and Gary to the ship. His hands writhed when he heard that Lissie had fled. He disappeared soon after, we assumed in search of her also. How far could a four-year-old go?

Caralee was crying with worry and desolation because she knew that Lissie was only trying to avoid being forced to leave everything she knew and loved. My wife stayed near the hut, nursing Miguel, and then she asked Miguel if he could show us where Lissie had gone.

He knew, all right. The picture he showed us said she was hiding in her tree. I ran to fetch her, but when I got there, it was to find that both Koosk and Dokófray had arrived before me. All three of us surrounded Lissie with loving arms, enfolding her with our grief. There was no point in further speeches about her going to Butterfly with her parents. I wouldn't say she was resigned to it, but with Dokófray there, I am sure it hit her that there could be no more rebellion.

I carried her back to the frozen bodies of the girls' parents. Then there was a reunion of goodbyes with Caralee hugging both newly awakened parents and Lissie again and again.

Gary was not so brazen with his demands anymore. Apparently, Jana and Gary finally saw that Dokófray was not going to allow their scheme to kidnap Miguel and force Caralee and me to go to Butterfly. So, with sagging hearts, they stopped arguing and instead just kissed and hugged.

When Dokófray's patience ended, and he ordered them up, Gary and Jana mounted their assigned spiders, and Lissie climbed up on Koosk for the very last time. Koosk, a normally black spider, now looked gray and straggly-haired. I wondered how long it would take him to recover from Lissie's absence. Seeing his misery softened my antipathy for the giant herd spider. I guess at that moment, I forgave him for biting me. He had actually done it only to help me, probably on Burska's orders.

Caralee and I were not welcome on this outward pilgrimage. Caralee had pleaded, but Dokófray had denied the request. Our goodbyes were said by the river near our dwelling, and then Caralee and I watched them heading out; Lissie turned to wave another goodbye. Her face was as streaked with tears as ours were. Caralee and I both cried out that we loved her and would see her when she visited.

Jana and Gary were only partially aware since they'd both been bitten after their final goodbye hugs. Herd spiders rarely bit humans, but when they did, ordered by Burska, no doubt, the fanged bite was swift. The girls' parents would have had no time for avoidance or for fear.

I knew the effect well since it hadn't been that long ago when Koosk had administered my bite during Caralee's birthing process. I'd been given only enough venom to calm me down and to allow the elderly herd spider to gift Caralee with a bite. Hers eased her pain and allowed her to deliver Miguel while laughing.

I recalled how a herd spider's bite was followed by a moment's sting as the venom shot up through the blood, but then, only numbness occurred. Jana and Gary would be able to ride their spiders to the ship, but they would scarcely remember their journey. They would certainly cause no trouble on the way.

I suspected that Lissie would also be bitten soon. In Miguel's vision, we had seen her walking onto the ship's ramp in a semi-drugged state. There would be no more attempts of escape for the little one. I hoped her bite would last her through blast-off. Like with Caralee's child birthing pain, providing a dull fog of numbness would be a blessing for her.

When the group's departure had become no more than a memory, Caralee and I were left to start our mourning. Our tears still flowed, although mine had lessened, not because I would miss the child less but because it was not in my nature to show my grief.

Lissie had been such a part of our lives from the moment of the invasion. To be without her boisterous and often whining complaints would be like finding a hole in one's arm — a painful wrong. Although, at first glance, it might look like we'd be feeling freedom from the heaviness of such a responsibility, her absence would be heartrending. She had become *our* child. I thought, at times, more ours than her parents. It would be impossible to glance down at the sandy area and not see Lissie in our memories, her stick busy carving pictures or digging huge sand castles with moats for all her river dragons.

Caralee would miss her mother, too. The two of them had been working on first aid, as well as stitchery; Caralee had told me at night what she'd done during the day, how she was proud of having absorbed new lessons of things she'd never been given the time to learn. Her mother had been talking about raising a child/children, as well. They were teachings Caralee had longed for and were now halted. It would be back to just us. No free babysitter, as Caralee had called her mother.

I would miss Gary, too. He had often been difficult, but sometimes he had shown me constructions I hadn't known before, like using notches to hold boards together since I didn't have nails or glue guns. He had offered simplistic solutions, shared his know how, and offered me some life discussions I found thought-provoking.

He spoke of government procedures, as when a settlement grew large enough to support officials. And we had discussed dealing with women. It wasn't that he'd wanted me to give in to Caralee more, but he'd given me advice on how to avoid conflict when executing decisions that I knew were right.

So, as I said, we were both grieving what we'd lost and the people we'd come to have relationships with.

Dokófray had told Caralee in a dream that Koosk would be moving in with us. He would become Miguel's protector after the ship lifted up.

I was about as thrilled with that as I'd been with Koosk sleeping with Lissie in our hut. Koosk and I still did not see eye-to-eye. I didn't trust him with Miguel. If I had the chance, I would tell that to Dokófray, but I knew I had as much chance of winning that battle as Lissie had in staying on Burska. I asked Caralee to ask Miguel if Koosk's presence would be welcome.

The moment the baby was put down on the ground, he crawled over to me. He propped himself up on my thigh bone, then wavering like a tree branch in the wind; he stood almost a moment before he collapsed against me. Of course, I was ready for his flop, holding him in my arms like the treasure he was.

Caralee sniffled, wiped her eyes and face, then leaned into me on the other side. My family may have grown a member smaller, but . . . then I remembered Alexandro.

Miguel laughed, then showed me a picture of more children. He named them for us: Miguel, Alexandro, Carolina, Angelica, and Fernando. Three boys and two girls. I exchanged a smile with Caralee. She no longer seemed to mind. Her fear was gone, both of child birthing and of raising them without the help of her mother.

But my question was supposed to be about Koosk, not our future family. Miguel's eyes turned to stare into mine. Apparently, that was harder to show, or at least, he seemed more uncertain.

He showed Koosk, a stronger, blacker Koosk, the herd spider grown healthy again, having finished his mourning. Koosk was shadowed by another. She was his wife. I think that was the image Miguel portrayed loosely. Speeta was pregnant, her abdomen dragging low with a large egg sack.

Koosk approached us, bowed low, and then drove his wife forward. She attempted a bow but really couldn't. Miguel continued the projection, showing both Koosk and Speeta taking over the bed where Lissie had slept.

"No," I ejected, but Miguel raised his hand and touched my lips. I think he was asking me not to speak.

A time progression occurred. Caralee was showing a much bigger stomach, Alexandro proclaiming his presence with a rippling in my wife's belly. Her hand covered his movement, and she smiled. Then Miguel showed us that Speeta no longer carried her egg sac. She'd deposited it up in a corner of the hut.

It was Caralee who cried out then. Miguel shook his head at his mother. Then he continued. The babies hatched, large numbers of them, maybe as many as fifty. Most of them left, crawling away on eight miniature legs. But three of them remained. Miguel identified them, placing the names inside our minds in some odd manner. Nartha, a deep brown male, was for Alexandro. Padora, a white female herd spider, was for Lissie, and Storma, a jet-black male, was Miguel's.

"But I thought Koosk was going to be your herd spider," I said, puzzled by it.

Miguel nodded his head. *Koosk will stay with me until Storma is ready, but Koosk is for you, as Speeta is for Mommy.*

That was the end of the images. Miguel opened his mouth to cry for his mommy and for milk. I stood and went for some Gorla fruit. Then, because Caralee asked for it, I brought her a branch of the Bedorka tree. It would provide us with water and with blessed sleep. Both seemed needed that evening.

Dokófray

Done. Trouble gone. No adjustment possible. Ship in space. Heading away. Bye, Lissie. Sadness.

Koosk gray. Need reestablishment. Miguel, Danuel. Danger gone. Worry still. Humans fragile. Spiders fragile. Much work ahead.

Burska say. Soon. Wake young, adaptable. Pairings. But not failures of before. They go on ship.

I fear. New element unsettles. Caralee need calm. But Burska say no. She say move forward. Always rush. Too fast.

Burskans tired. Much energy utilization of ship movement. Must rest. All. I return to ship. Rest.

Caralee

We had eaten of the Bedorka. Danuel and I were ready to crawl into bed when Koosk arrived with his wife, Speeta. I felt Danuel puff up, ready to give battle. I shook my head, as did Miguel. We both sought to calm Danuel. I gave him a smile and a shoulder shrug, reminding him that Burska had given us a warning of what was to come.

But Miguel carried the moment with his "Da da."

Danuel had almost given up, trying to get the baby to say that instead of Fa Fa. My husband's smile was radiant. Forgetting the approach of the two herd spiders, he picked up Miguel and hugged and kissed him. No question that Danuel was thrilled by his son's acknowledgement. That was good because it gave me the opportunity to say what I needed to say.

Koosk was still bowing to us. I waved him up, but Speeta hung back, cowering behind her male. I doubted that she had spent any time near humans. We seemed to frighten her.

"Welcome home, Koosk," I said. "Miguel has told us that you and Speeta will be joining us in the hut. It is harder to accept such newness because, like you, we are grieving for Lissie. To see you there without her is difficult for both of us, but we know it is what Burska wants. She has shown us that you and Speeta will occupy Lissie's bed each night.

"Speeta, I see your egg sac. I also am carrying an egg. Only one. Human babies are big. Miguel says that you will soon harbor your babies on the wall of our hut. You are welcome to do so when the time comes."

Danuel said nothing. His eyes skimmed over the new herd spider. He shuddered. "Caralee?" he questioned, then fell silent.

I knew what he was thinking. This was not something we welcomed. Baby spiders crawling about? And yet, Miguel had shown us that image. We knew that this was something we must endure.

I ignored Danuel's interruption, barging on. "But now, we are all tired. Let us sleep," I said, concluding my speech with a very ungracious huge yawn.

Danuel, with Miguel in his arms, and I staggered sleepily into the hut. The Bedorka's water had hit us more gradually than usual. Perhaps Burska's had slowed it to allow for my herd spider greeting. But once inside, we practically melted into the bed, sleeping without waking the whole night. If the herd of spiders joined us in the hut, we never heard them. They weren't there in the morning.

Miguel woke us, of course. His greed for breakfast was a daily occurrence. Babies, apparently, have no patience for late rising. The expression *the crack of dawn* was probably originated by a new parent, cracking open sleepy eyes for a cranky baby's demands.

Thankfully, feeding Miguel required almost no effort. Mother Nature knew just what she was doing when she provided a mother's instant feeding system.

Meanwhile, Danuel got out of bed and made his way to the bushes, then returned with a couple of Gorla fruits. Miguel, although he insisted on milk, still wanted his share of the fruit. Danuel started chewing, preparing for the moment Miguel was ready for the chewed Gorla paste. Not a moment later, Danuel's mouth opened for some sweet fruit paste. He was almost as insatiable for that as for my milk nowadays. If Danuel didn't chew fast enough, Miguel squawked like a parrot I'd once seen in a pirate movie.

With our little monster's feeding completed, I did my thing in the bushes, then washed my face with the river water we kept in a discarded turtle shell. On Burska, turtles outgrew their shells and abandoned them. We were lucky to have a more than an adequate supply. Who needed conventional dishes when they could use items with such striking colors? Each shell was a work of art, something that probably belonged in a museum. But our checker board, bowls, roofing, and a Miguel bathtub were all supplied with these multicolored shells, leaving us surrounded in beauty.

After Danuel brought Miguel outside, I bathed the baby then covered his bottom with leaves. They were pretty efficient for preventing leaks, but every parent will tell you that nothing prevents a flood. Good thing the river waters had formed our own personal inlet for bathing.

After that was done, Danuel looked at me, and I at him, and we broke out into laughter because we'd just realized we had nothing to do. The hut was good. My sewing projects were done. No Lissie to play with. No one to tell stories to or listen to hers. What were we supposed to do with all our spare time? I guess Danuel and I just should have kicked back and relaxed, but we really didn't know how to do that.

"Do you want to go swimming," Danuel asked. But it was a chilly, overcast day, and swimming didn't appeal.

"A trip to the orchard?"

I shook my head to that, too. That reminded me of Lissie too much. Lissie and the farmhouse I wasn't allowed to visit, the one where my parents had lived.

Danuel and I had just decided to take a walk and explore an area we'd never gone to when the aliens popped up: Flistercrokta, Dokófray, then Turndaloff with his funny hat. Others came, too. Maybe five who we'd seen on our medical trip to the ship, but never been given their names.

"What's up, Dokófray?" Danuel asked.

I wished he'd been more formal. It was always wise not to antagonize those who had the power to turn you into a fence post.

Miguel broke into song like he did with the herd spiders. Almost at once, we had a huge crowd of spiders surrounding us, with Koosk and Speeta in front.

"Good," Dokófray. "We go now."

"Hold it," Danuel said, his voice wisely calm and low, but his hand raised as if the palm could halt whatever was about to transpire.

"More information needed, Dokófray," Danuel said, copying the alien's syntax.

"Miguel, not tell? We go wake up at six. Three pairs."

I couldn't help slightly raising my voice. I was just too excited to be calm. "You're going to wake up some of our friends?"

Of course, I couldn't say I'd actually had many friends. Living so far from school, I'd never really had the chances that Danuel had to intermingle or form relationships. And then there was Lissie. Mom always needed me to watch her while she did her nursing job at the hospital. Something like that really cuts into fun time.

But no Lissie now. I wanted to jump and shout, to skip around and dance, but I stifled it and thought *calm. Quiet atmosphere.* All that stuff which was short of impossible for a sixteen-year-old, even one who was pregnant and carrying a baby on her hip.

Danuel turned and smiled, then broke out in laughter. "Yeah, more teen beauty queen than mother figure," he kidded me. Then he curved his arm around my head and slobbered kisses on my cheek and lips. That made Miguel laugh almost as hard.

"Ma ma," he cried out, but I knew he wasn't asking for milk. He was full. He was naming me, calling to me.

I lifted him higher and kissed him, too. Perhaps that was all he wanted, an inclusion in our group kiss?

But the moment my lips touched his head, the images began. The garbage dump shacks where my mother had been. The standing pretzels, our classmates, and younger kids. So many of them. Had they all been sent to one room? Were there more of them?

Miguel squinted his eyes, sorting through faces until we saw him choosing six. How did he know who to pick? Wouldn't it have been better to ask Danuel who'd gone to school with most of those kids?

The images switched. We saw us leading them to our river site. Where were the new people supposed to sleep? Surely not in our hut. It was already too crowded. But Miguel wasn't answering such questions, only showing us scenes from our future.

I didn't know any of the kids. Danuel didn't seem to either. I thought they might be older, closer to the age of legal pairing. Is that why they'd been chosen?

The scene shifted. The young people were building huts at a walking distance but not super close. The huts looked good to me. It looked like the kids were already pairing. There was some hugging going on.

The vision cleared and Dokófray was telling us to mount up. I knew I was supposed to ride Speeta, but she was carrying an egg sac. Dokófray called another over, and I mounted the female assigned. Danuel climbed up on Koosk, not happy about it, according to his snarly face, but he was holding Miguel, who had probably instructed him to do so.

The aliens didn't ride the herd of spiders, however. They drifted along as if they were wind-blown seed pods. "How do they do that?" I asked, speaking out loud.

No one answered, probably because no one knew. The aliens had probably invented another technological wonder, or maybe they'd had it all along, but before, when I'd been injured, they'd ridden something that Danuel described as motorcycles that floated. If the aliens had such technologies, why didn't they let us use them instead of the very slow-moving herd spiders? (Of course, I knew that complaint was ridiculous since herd spiders could gallop and were probably not doing so because of Danuel holding the baby and me being pregnant.)

We traveled all day, stopping for fruit and some Kiginoa. It reminded me of the first time we'd dug up some. Lissie had shown us how to harvest it. I sprinkled some tears over the piece we replanted.

That night, we slept on the ground as we had done so often before. It was not as comfortable as the leafy reed bed Danuel had built for us, but we were young. Our backs didn't hurt yet. My mother had complained about hers when she'd been forced to sleep on the ground. With that memory. My tears came again, but I rationalized that they were only hormones from my pregnancy. At least that's what I told Danuel, but I don't think he was fooled.

We arrived the next day. Waking up the girls was first on the agenda for some reason. I certainly didn't like that because they oohed and aahed over Danuel's muscles. I know they were drug-fevered, but . . .

There were three of them, all of them really pretty: Bonnie with long, straight black hair that was super shiny, and whenever she flipped it, not a single hair fell out of place. Her nose was perfect, her lips the right shade of pinkish red, and her dark eyes were almost almond-shaped.

Patsy was a blonde, small and petite, but plump in the places that guys wanted plumpness in girls. Her eyes were her best feature. They were baby blue with lashes that were so long they looked artificial.

Third was Sally. She acted shyer than the other two. Her hair was long and wavy in a brownish hue that held streaks of gold. Of course, she was also pretty.

And all of the girls were wearing tight jeans with long-sleeved shirts. They looked fashionable and stylish, unlike me in my spider web stitched dress over the knee-length pants I'd fashioned from Corumba tree leaves. I bet they'd had hair trims recently — at least just before they went into stasis.

When Dokófray woke up the males, there was no oohing and aahing over me, unlike the very flirtatious way the girls had processed Daniel. I guess a woman holding a baby on her hip and showing the bulge of another on the way put teenage boys off. I wanted to yell out, "Hey, I'm only sixteen, not forty, but that would have made me sound desperate, and I wasn't. I already had the most handsome husband in the world. (But the way they ignored me wasn't good for my ego.)

The first one was named Lance. He looked like one of the football jocks in old Earth movies. His body was trimmed, and I think he probably worked out. He was fair-haired with longish hair that kept drooping into his eyes. I bet the girls went wild over the way he tossed his head to keep it out of his eyes.

Leonardo was next. I liked his name, but that was about all. He wore a sneer like others wore clothes. As my mother used to say, he looked like someone with a chip on his shoulder. I never knew if that was a potato chip, a poker chip, or a computer chip. Mother never told me. Leonardo was handsome, I suppose, but he looked like a bully. I bet he'd be the first to mock someone who took a tumble or stuttered. Leonardo's appearance was average, with black hair and deep blue eyes. Unlike the other two, who wore simple jeans and tees, Leonardo was wearing all black.

Matthew was the one I liked the most. He had gentle brown eyes, and he winked at me. But that wasn't why I thought he was the nicest. He looked thoughtful like he'd be a person who would help the stutterer that Leonardo made fun of. I bet Matthew would give a guy who tumbled, a hand up.

Danuel, touching our mind link, raised an eyebrow. "Competition," he asked. I just smiled and shook my head.

Thankfully, none of the newbies were afraid of herd spiders. They didn't know these were the wild kind, instead of the tame ones like my parents raised. Still in a kind of fog, like my parents had been, the six climbed up on top of the herd spiders without any argument. Bonnie cried out that she needed help, and Danuel rushed over to give her a hand. I noticed that Bonnie, who was supposed to be paired with Matthew, was still giving Danuel a flirtatious eye.

Danuel helped the other two girls as well and then got up on Koosk. He was still hanging beside them, making sure they didn't need anything.

"Miguel," I whispered to the baby. Sure enough, he was awake and eyeing me. "Could you ask the herd spiders to move so we can get them into couples? You know, Bonnie next to Matthew, Sally next to Lance, and Patsy with Leonardo? That way, they could get to know each other quicker."

Miguel stared up at me, his head tilting a bit. He blew a bubble out the side of his mouth. I wasn't sure what that meant, but the next minute, Danuel was sitting beside me, Koosk pushing his wiry spider body tightly against my leg.

"Wow! What was that about?" Danuel asked. "I was just trying to give some explanations to the girls when Koosk took off and galloped me over here. Do you need help with the baby?"

"Da da," Miguel cried out, holding his arms out like he couldn't wait to get away from me. It made me feel bad. Had I made Miguel angry when I'd asked him to do some spider juggling?"

I didn't answer Danuel, but I could feel my face flaming with embarrassment. Danuel was quiet for a minute, then he jumped down from Koosk and jerked me off my spider. "Don't you ever think anything like that? I adore you, my wife. I cherish the ground you walk on. I wouldn't look at one of those girls for a stack of construction books or a locker full of tools. You're my wife, and I won't have you being jealous. You hear me?"

I heard him all right, and so did all the herd spiders and our new guests. If a blush could get blushier, mine did. I'd gone from tomato face to beet juice purple. I sank my face into Danuel's web-knitted shirt and sucked in the smell that was Danuel: security, togetherness, love, friendship, my everything. Yet, in all Danuel's words, I noticed he hadn't said anything about me being the most beautiful. Pregnancy plump and hormonally challenged. That was me.

He turned my head to look down into my eyes. "You silly goose," he said. "You already know I think you're the most beautiful girl in all of Burska. Haven't I said that a thousand times already?"

The tears started then. He was right. I was a goose. A floppy-footed, blubbery waddler with a pillow for a waist.

"Koosk, tell the others we need a break. My wife and I need a few minutes of quality time. We'll be back in a bit. Oh, and Koosk, make sure the six wake-ups don't go anywhere. And here. I do trust you with Miguel. He's your responsibility, Burska says," Danuel said, shoving the baby into the spider's top arms.

I wasn't ready to go that far and opened my mouth to argue about that, but Danuel picked me up in his arms and, carrying me bride-like, marched off into the woods, leaving everyone behind us.

A few kisses, well, a lot of kisses later, I was feeling much better. And then there were the images Danuel shoved into my head, images that showed his love and the way he felt about me.

"You will always be my sweetheart," Danuel said as he squeezed me hard one last time. "Let's go see how Koosk is dealing with Miguel. Oh, and I was pretty authoritarian. I guess I need to apologize for that."

I didn't respond except to giggle, and then I took his hand so we could walk back.

I think that little episode established some things quite clearly. Not only the fact that Danuel was taken and the girls needed to keep their hands and flirty eyes off him, but that the herd spiders did exactly what Daniel wanted; he had taken the initiative to show that he was the one in charge, a fact that no one challenged.

We rode steadily until the fog-darkness defeated Sir Vagabond and Lady Hobo, the two moons that had been making an effort to light up the sky that night. Then we stopped, dined on Gorla fruit, which the newcomers had to be convinced was safe enough to eat, then did our best to find places that were stone free for sleeping.

Bonnie, Sally, and Patsy tried to join us, perhaps thinking they were safest near Danuel, but Koosk and the other herd spiders dissuaded them. Seeing that avenue cut off, the girls ended up laying down next to the guys, although I noticed that they all clunked together by gender. The males didn't even have the sense to form an outer ring around the females. Danuel would have thought of that. He'd always put the needs of Lissie and me first.

I pointed that out to Danuel, thanking him again for how sweet he'd been when Lissie and I were so scared and lost in those first days.

"Only then?" he asked. "Not now?"

I fake-slugged him for that. Then I kissed him intensely, with the kind of kiss that usually ended up delightfully, but not, unfortunately, when we were surrounded by so many eyes. Koosk, for one, lay no more than two feet away, his eyes steadfastly open, so we never knew if he was asleep or awake. He had taken Danuel's words to heart. The baby lay swaddled in his multiple arms, as happy as Miguel had always been when sleeping between us.

I thought about being jealous about how easily we'd been replaced, but I was much too tired. Pregnancy sapped energy. My eyes closed, and I slept securely wrapped up in Danuel's arms.

We arrived home the next day in time to harvest some more Gorla fruit, enough for us and the newcomers. We also dug up some Kiginoa root. The latter was rather ugly to look at, so it wasn't easy to convince the six of them to try a piece of the root, but they finally did, then decided that they wanted more. Of course, that wasn't a possibility. One piece was all that was needed.

"Hey man," Leonardo said. "Don't be like that. All we've had all day was a fruit at lunch and one just now. We're hungry."

"Yeah," everyone said, backing him up.

"I could use some backup here, Dokófray," Danuel said, but the alien had taken off the moment he'd finished waking up the newbies. He was probably back up on his ship.

But at least Danuel's words quieted the group.

"Hey, man, don't get weird on us," Leonardo said. "Okay, we'll wait for tomorrow, but the grub needs to improve, right?" he said, checking out the opinions of those around him.

Danuel did his best to ignore that. He drew in a long breath, then exhaled slowly. "There are certain rules the aliens have given us."

"Aliens?" Bonnie said, sliding closer to Leonardo. "What aliens?"

Leonardo gave her a long, cool look. I wasn't sure he was as taken with her as she was with him. His eyes traveled over Sally and Patsy, assessing, perhaps deciding which girl he'd focus on. It was obvious that Leonardo planned to rule the group, and I could see him plotting to gain the attention of whichever girl he favored most.

I moved closer, carrying Miguel in my arms. Koosk followed, his eyes scanning the group, probably doing his own assessment of the danger. Speeta had come out to join us. She was still heavy with the egg sac, I hoped the group would treat her with respect. I introduced her and made sure they knew Koosk.

"Is he the lead spider?" Patsy asked.

I nodded. "He is also Miguel's and Danuel's bodyguard. Speeta will be mine soon once she deposits the egg sac."

"Eww," Bonnie said, rolling her eyes. "I heard there can be hundreds of baby spiders crawling out of that. Not here, I hope," she said, looking all around us in case there were other egg sacs nearby.

"If you are lucky, if you earn the loyalty of him or her, one of those babies might become your friend, your own bodyguard and mount. I am honored that Speeta has chosen me."

I didn't know if that was true exactly. Had Speeta chosen to be with us, or was she just obeying Burska? I hope it was the former.

Speeta stepped closer. An arm reached out to touch me. A spider's caress was never an unpleasant experience. Their pads might be hard enough to gallop on, but when they used them to make contact, the foot cushions were soft as velvet. I couldn't explain it, but having been raised with herd spiders, I knew it for a fact.

Speeta's tender stroke was a mere whisp of a touch, unsure in nature and extremely timid. I reached up to scratch the parts of her mandible that always seemed to itch. Speeta was so receptive to that she began to purr. What was really bizarre is that inside the sac, the unborn spiders all hummed in unison.

"Gross," said Bonnie.

"Not at all," Sally disagreed. "I think it's beautiful." She sat up on her knees to observe better, then smiled as if it were music she'd longed to hear.

Sally became my favorite of the six at that moment.

Danuel

I had lots to tell the newcomers. I'd even thought out a proper sequence, but things just got jumbled around, Leonardo throwing in complaints, Caralee talking about the herd spiders. I just lost my whole repertoire, to be truthful.

But I remembered how stuff like this had happened to the aliens when we'd first arrived on their ship. They'd wanted to drill us on protocol and we'd demanded togetherness and a bathroom. So, I shrugged my shoulders, smiled at my dear wife, and said, "Time to bunk down. See you in the morning."

"Good night, Danuel," Bonnie simpered.

Koosk growled at her. I'd never seen him do that. It startled all of us.

"If you know what's good for you, Bonnie, you will be more respectful to my wife," Danual snapped.

She paled, understanding the threat perfectly. Matthew stood up and walked over to her. "The baby said I'm supposed to be in charge of you. I don't know why, and I sure don't understand how a baby can be talking, especially when he's not old enough to be talking, but . . ."

Bonnie looked up at Danuel, giving it one more shot. "I thought you were in charge, Danuel. I don't understand," she said, ignoring Matthew's extended hand.

"Okay. I wanted to deal with this tomorrow, but I'll just let it flow right now. Things aren't what you think. Beatnik is not Beatnik. The planet is called Burska, and she's sentient . . ."

Leonardo was shaking his head and making the crazy sign.

"Stop it unless you need a bit of spider venom in your arm. Koosk's bite is nasty," Danuel warned. "I know from experience.

"Anyway, here's the part Bonnie was asking about. Burska assigned Caralee to me. She was only fifteen back then, but I think you guys are older, right?"

They started telling him their ages. The guys went first: Matthew, Leonardo, and Lance were all eighteen. Then the girls got into it. Bonnie, still pouting over Danuel's words, said, "Who cares? I'm eighteen, old enough to do whatever I want. Patsy went next. She said she was seventeen. Sally said, "Me, too, but if we've been in stasis as they tell us, aren't we all a year older now?"

"Maybe," Leonardo said, "if you believe them."

Leonardo kept reaffirming my opinion. He was jerk city all the way. But it was interesting to know. Did it count to be a year older if they were in stasis? Had their bodies aged? Daniel and I had been awake the whole time, so it was still valid that Danuel was the eldest at twenty, and I was still the youngest at sixteen. But I was close. It wasn't like I was a Lissie to their ancient.

But back to Bonnie's question. Burska has paired you guys up. Sally, you're with Lance. Patsy, you're with Leonardo. Bonnie, you're with Matthew."

Danuel shifted and pulled me up closer to him. He took a moment to tickle Miguel's tummy, which, as usual, made him laugh.

"Don't bother arguing with me about that. I'm just telling you what the planet demands. You can fight it if you like. I don't care. But I warn you, there are always consequences in resistance.

"Later, when you have settled down, you can construct your own huts because this is permanent. Burska has ordered that you stay here, the same order she gave Caralee and me. You can either be happy about it or go back to the shacks where you've been in stasis this last year. As I told you before, all the adults are gone. It's just us and the new ones the aliens will wake in the future.

"Now, Caralee and I are bedding down, so good night."

As we started to walk away, I looked back. Koosk was eyeing Leonardo in a not-very-friendly manner. "Koosk?" I called out. One more growl at Leonardo, and Koosk trotted after us. Speeta was already beside me. She rubbed Koosk with one of her arms, and he wrapped two or three arms around her. Together, we all walked toward our hut, very glad to be home.

Danuel

The next day was rough. The girls were fighting over the guys. The males were fighting each other, and none of them would listen.

Caralee tried to separate Sally from the others, but Lance wouldn't permit it. Caralee then invited Lance to come with her, too, so she could show both of them how she was sewing the herd spider web into clothing. Lance wasn't interested, and then the other girls drifted over to see what Sally was being shown. *Bicker, bicker, bicker,* according to Caralee, and I could feel her frustration clear across the divide, where I'd taken the guys to show them the location for their huts.

"Yeah, and why can't we build these huts closer to you? Is Caralee a screamer when you two . . ."

I would have slugged him if I hadn't spotted aliens up on the overlook watching. I pointed up there, telling the guys that it was Burska and the aliens who made sure all rules and decisions were followed, but none of the gents could see the aliens, so I got that same finger motion from Leonardo, acting like he thought I was crazy.

Of course, that reminded me of what he'd just said about Caralee, which gave me a slow burn . . but then, it also reminded me of the training we'd endured on the alien ship. Calm environment, festive voices . . .

Stuff like that was a lot more difficult when jerks were taunting me. So, I dropped the subject, shrugged my shoulders, and retreated. Kind of a coward's way of doing things, but I recalled Flistercrokta doing the same thing whenever he found us too difficult to work with.

"Wait," Matthew called out. "Is this for real? You and Caralee have been here for a whole year?"

"Yes. More than a year now.

"With no one else?"

"Well, no. If you really want the story, I'll tell you, but we might as well sit down and try to be friendly."

At first, only Matthew sat down in the dirt, ready to hear the tale, but then Lance joined us, and Leonardo, still refusing to be even semi-amenable, stood over to the side, his hand on his hips in a *I don't believe a word of this stance.*

I ignored him. Chances are, if he continued with his attitude, he'd become a frozen pole soon. And maybe returned to stasis.

While I was telling the two guys about the raid on the farmhouse, the girls came over. They sat down, making it like a campfire circle. I patted the ground for Caralee to join me, and she did, sitting in front, then leaning back against me. She was holding the baby, who'd fallen asleep, no doubt bored with her discussion about making clothing out of spider webs.

The newbies' eyes got bigger when I spoke of us getting captured and ending up on the alien ship. I skipped over a few spots like Caralee wetting herself, but I did explain about three-year-old Lissie's often bad attitude and how she liked to call out *bananas* whenever we were being quizzed.

"Where is she now?" Sally asked, her eyes already searching for the mischievous imp.

"She's with her parents," Caralee said. "We really miss her."

"Yeah, and where are her parents?" Leonardo wanted to know.

I continued the tale, skipping parts and darting around a bit. "Caralee's and Lissie's mother and father were wakened up first, but it was discovered that the fruit didn't sustain them. Burska ordered them back to the ship. The alien loaded all the adults and our little sister, and the ship was lifted up into space. According to the Caralee's father, they were headed for a planet named Butterfly."

"You sure can make up good stories," Leonardo said.

"You rude," Dokófray said. "You I return."

Sally and Bonnie screamed. Patsy fainted. The other guys didn't move. They seemed frozen.

"Danuel, tell truth. You ridicule. Danuel and Caralee try help and give advice. You no listen. Why?"

Matthew was the first to recover his tongue. "You are an alien, not a herd spider?"

Dokófray looked at Matthew but didn't answer. "I give you two days. If he still obstinate, take back, choose other."

Caralee

Patsy was sitting up by then, recovered from her faint. Sally had helped her up, not one of the guys. Of course, her mate was supposed to be Leonardo, so that might be the problem. Maybe Dokófray would give her a different mate, a better one. I crossed my fingers.

"No," Dokófray said, giving me his full attention. "She mate. If he goes, she must."

"But, I didn't cause trouble," Patsy said.

"Talk sense into mulish head."

Dokófray walked closer to Danuel and me. He looked down at Miguel, meeting his eyes. "Sing, Miguel. Sing for Herd spiders."

As if Miguel had an on button, the high-pitched humming started up at once. Koosk and Speeta were first to join us, but in a minute, twenty herd spiders surrounded us, and then thirty, and as we watched, more of them came crowding around.

"Miguel is Spider Hopper. Alexandro will be Judge. Danuel First Father. Caralee, First Mother. All bow to them. They lead. You follow. Maybe get spider. Maybe not. But spiders bite. You do what Danuel and Caralee say. This Burska rule. She say."

Then, looking down at me, he said. "I hold Miguel?"

Perhaps I was too slow in my response, or maybe it was just easier for Danuel to pass the baby to Dokófray. I only know that an eye blink later, the alien was holding our baby. Of course, he'd done so before, but . . .

"I not hurt Miguel. Never. You know, Caralee. You need to let go. Others here be with Miguel sometimes. Good for him. Good for you."

I nodded. Danuel had also spoken of my holding on too much like the time I'd panicked when he took Miguel with him. It was his right. I knew I was in the wrong to want to have the baby with me at all times. But it was hard. My parents were gone. Lissie was gone. Miguel was all I had left."

"No. Wrong. You have Danuel. Always." Dokófray said, flapping his two upper arms at me as if they were finger scolding me.

I nodded. Dokófray was right. I looked down at my hands, writhing with worry. It was a silly habit, like forgetting to breathe when I panicked.

Danuel's arms encircled me. He tightened them so that I could hardly move, hardly breathe. "Always, my love. Always," he said.

A tear fell. I did that a lot. Pregnancy or mourning is one of those.

"Remember in the woods?" Danuel asked. "Do I need to show you those images again? Have you forgotten?"

I wiggled until he released me a tiny bit, then I moved my lips to kiss his chin. It was all I could reach with him holding me so tightly.

"Good," Dokófray said. "You do not let new people upset you. Alexandro is important. They not."

Then he handed the baby back to us, placing him down in my lap. "You listen to Miguel. He know. He talk to Burska."

Dokófray turned back to the others. "You do what Danuel and Caralee say. No argument. We watch. We see. If need, we return. You pretzel man again." Dokófray turned to look at me. Then his probiscis unfurled in his full-out belly laugh. "Pretzel man. I like expression. I remember."

If someone blinked, they missed him disappearing. One moment, he was there unfurling his probiscis, then gone.

Caralee

I had the strangest dream. Miguel was older, maybe ten or so. He was riding a spider I didn't know and galloping beside my Speeta. Miguel and I were laughing together, enjoying our outing. I asked him what spider hopping meant, and he told me. Just that simple, after all this time of wondering.

It is hopping from spider to spider, of course, Mom like this. He stood up on the back of the spider, then jumped onto the back of another who'd come up beside his. But he wasn't done showing off because before I could call out for him to stop and tell him how dangerous this was, he'd left the current spider and was traveling across the back of four more. I was crying out, "Stop, stop!" when he returned to my side.

It is what I was meant to do. Do not fear for me.

Of course, I am scared. I love you. I can't bear to see you get hurt. To fall off might . . .

Do you think they would allow me to be hurt? I am theirs. They protect me.

Yes, but what if a spider ducks away to avoid a tree or trips over something? I mind sent.

Then another would take his place. I am safest on top of the herd spiders' backs, Mom. There will never be danger there.

How do you know? Are you communicating with them?

Always. I am the Spider Hopper of their minds, as well. We are one, bonded through Burska. You could walk their minds, too, if you reached out. Koosk could guide you. He is always receptive to your reach. Both you and Dad.

I can never do the things you do, Miguel. You are special.

As are you.

The dream faded. Speeta slipped away, and I found myself in my bed, lying beside my husband.

It was only a dream, I told myself, but Miguel opened his eyes and stared into mine, and I knew then that I had seen the future.

Sleep, Mommy, baby Miguel said, and I closed my eyes and dropped back into sleep.

In the morning, when I told Danuel about the dream, he accepted it as truth. "Of course," he said. "We should have seen it all along. Everything Miguel said makes perfect sense until the end when he says that you and I could communicate with them as well."

I don't know if Miguel was listening to the conversation. He was pretty much inside his feeding frenzy at that moment, slurping milk like he'd been starved for a week.

But Koosk was sitting up in the strange way that herd spiders sat. It made no sense how a rounded abdomen could balance itself to perform a platform of stability, but the spiders did that on occasion, mimicking human habits, I presumed.

When he felt my eyes on him, he stood up and came closer. *Yes, Danuel. I can hear you. I am ready to connect with you whenever you wish, whenever you muster up enough faith in Miguel to know that you can.*

I did not hear Koosk's words to Danuel, but I saw it reflected in his eyes and read from my husband's mind that Koosk was speaking to him. With the wonder of it, I gasped. The small sound broke their link. Miguel looked up at me, bubbled an exclamation point, then opened his mouth and laughed.

Too shocked by the morning's events, I bent down and kissed Miguel. "I love you, my little baby, whether you ride Spiders or not. I love you."

His baby hand reached up and patted my cheek.

Danuel

The world looks different after enlightenment pricks you with the claws of discovery. Did I accept what had just happened? Could I accept? Fruits that offered complete sustenance, spidery aliens, stasis invoking year-long sleep, herd spiders that mind-linked . . . my disbelief had long since evaporated with the daily turbulence of weird. I felt, sometimes, as if the ground beneath me threatened to swallow me up with newness. Or perhaps I might sink because everything I'd once believed had been churned over like greenhouse soil at the end of a harvest.

Koosk could speak with me, and I with him. In fact, he'd said he awaited my willingness to do so. Me, who herd spiders, constantly rejected. How could that be true? Yet, the way Koosk's principal eyes had stared into mine, the knowingness there, I had to accept it. Another change, another realization that we were Burska's to mold as she desired.

My thought process was halted by a cry from Bonnie; She was fighting with Matthew. It was time to begin training the newbies. But why couldn't Flistercrokta descend from the ship and take over? Why did I have to crack through the just wokens' resistance and spur on their positive growth? I doubted I was up for the challenge. I could barely maintain peace with Caralee at times. Didn't the aliens and Burska realize I was faulty, not the right First Father for their needs?

Koosk had followed me outside. He brushed up against me, the petting of his hairy legs against my spider-silk pants created a vibration of sorts. I took a step sideways.

"Koosk," I said, but then stopped. What was I wanting to say? Don't touch me? Don't imply we were now friends. Don't make me question my sanity.

Two of his arms reached out to pull me back. His principal eyes dug deep into my brain with a fierce mind link that I couldn't reject. Imprinting. That's what he was doing. How did I know that? What did it mean? Where was Miguel to translate this invasion into my . . . My what, my soul, my good sense?

Caralee came skipping out of the hut, looking prepregnant. Where had she gotten this sudden burst of energy? Why did she look so rosy-cheeked and happy?

Bonnie screamed. I looked over to see Matthew walking away, shaking his head. He looked dejected, horrified with having to deal with Bonnie. I felt great sympathy for him. It seemed like Bonnie should have been matched with Leonardo. They deserved each other.

Caralee had come up behind me, her arms encircling my waist. Feeling her whole body pressed against mine, I wondered where Miguel was. He was usually hip-attached or in her arms.

But then Speeta came into sight. She had Miguel in her arms. The herd spider was tickling the baby with her probiscis. That was a new one to me. It made me the slightest bit uncomfortable, but then I relaxed into it. Miguel was always safe with the herd spiders. Miguel had told us that himself. But then, a new awareness hit me. Caralee had relinquished the baby. She had allowed someone else to absorb a moment of responsibility. She had listened to Dokófray.

Koosk still stood beside me, watching me. I knew what he wanted. I saw that as Caralee had needed to let go, I was being forced to let down my guard.

"Okay, Koosk. I am ready. I think."

The arms came out, enwrapping me. Then Koosk and I blended until I was herd spider and human all at once. The oneness was both alarming and fulfilling. I teetered between backing away and releasing this sharing and freely accepting it. But that was what this was all about. Like Lissie's fantasy drawbridges, Caralee and I both needed to lower our ramps. We had to completely accept Burska and her herd spiders.

I gave in, and the sudden download from Koosk opened me.

Miguel

I tell Dokófray and Burska what happen. They happy. Mommy and Daddy one step closer. Mommy see dream. Mommy obey Dokófray. She give me to Speeta.

Mommy tell Daddy. Daddy see. He folds in Koosk. Accept. Now aware. Herd Spider-like people. He understand.

Now, new people. Not easy. I tell Dokófray help Daddy. Daddy doubts. Koosk helps. Not good. Burska tell Dokófray. Daddy asks for Flistercrokta. He come. Both come. Both help.

I let loose. Feel good. Speeta not know how clean. Mommy, Daddy I cry. Mommy come fast. She see problem. Good. I feel good. Now clean.

I want Gorla fruit. I cry. Open mouth. Mommy sees. I not talk mind. She know need. She feed paste. Good. I happy. I smile.

I watch new people. Tell Koosk. Many problem. Burskan, come, I say. Koosk drop long thing, prob thing. Big word. I see in mind. But not know word. I listen more. Learn. I want learn. Talk.

Leonardo. Big word. I learn. He come. Mean face. I not like. I tell Koosk. I like Patsy. I want her stay. Not Leonardo.

Patsy come. She make small talk. I smile. She say ooh. She smile. Leonardo looks. He like Patsy. I know. He want Patsy happy. He coo. I smile, Leonardo. He stay, maybe.

Caralee

I didn't give Miguel back to Speeta after changing him. I fed him some Gorla fruit paste, then held him up so he could see all around. He liked to do that. He seemed especially interested in the newcomers. I guess new faces are intriguing for a baby to analyze.

Patsy and Leonardo walked towards us, he with his usual sneer and she with eyes full of tenderness for the baby in my arms. Miguel was never shy. He beamed up at the petite blonde, probably intrigued by the way the sun played with her hair, making it glitter like gold. When she began to coo at him, he burst into a four-toothed full smile.

I glanced over at Leonardo, standing a couple of feet back; his eyes were on Patsy more than Miguel, but he wasn't sneering, at least.

"Did you ever think about having children?" I asked Leonardo, watching his eyes for a reaction to my question. He was good at the Poker face, but he couldn't help the reaction. I'd surprised him, whether from my addressing him or from the question, I couldn't be sure. He tried to blanket it, but I knew Miguel would catch whatever stray thoughts he'd released. I'd ask the baby later about whether he thought Leonardo could ever be trusted enough to join us.

I didn't have to wait. Miguel poured his thoughts into my mind. *Leonardo likes Patsy. He thinks of leaving. But Patsy keeps him here. We must watch. I assign herd spider to him, on guard. No leave.*

I forgot myself and spoke out loud. "But there's no place to go. Burska won't let Leonardo leave."

"You talking to the planet," Leonardo asked. "She couldn't stop me, could she? A planet has no hands or feet and no weapons."

"She have us," Dokófray said, walking up behind Leonardo. "You want proof? Danuel not tell you? Maybe visit ship. We put in room. Then you see."

"What ship?" Leonardo asked, his eyes checking out the sky like he could see the ship.

"Believe me, it's up there," Danuel said, lining up behind me, so he could play peek-a-boo with Miguel.

"Your son is so cute," Patsy said. "How old is he?"

Did she not see that we were in the middle of a confrontation? But I responded anyway. "We don't really know. No calendars, you know. Probably about ten months, but that's just a guess. He has started crawling and even tries to stand up. He has four teeth now. What do you think?"

Patsy seemed surprised I'd ask her. She gulped and looked down. "Well, I think that's probably pretty accurate, but he has a really long attention span, and I've seen him move his head to look at something you mention. That usually comes much later.

I smiled. She seemed a wealth of information. "Have you been caretaking babies, then?" I asked, remembering how the students all had to spend time with little children so they'd be more knowledgeable about their care.

She nodded and asked if she could hold Miguel. I glanced back at Danuel, but he was already okaying it mentally. *Patsy's no risk, right, Koosk?*

Wow. Buddies now. A day ago they'd been, if not enemies, then avoidance prone.

I handed Miguel to Patsy, kissing his cheek as I did so. He seemed happy about the exchange. He raised his hand to pat her on the cheek. That seemed to be his new favorite thing to do. Had he copied that from the herd spiders? It was something I'd noticed that they did when greeting each other.

Miguel was laughing. Leonardo looked over. "Patsy," he said. "Do you want to have one with me?"

I think he meant it sarcastically, but Patsy considered the question a minute. She studied him, then said, "That's depends, Leonardo. Would you be a good father?"

I felt so out of place right then. Those two needed privacy, but maybe stating such things publicly was safer for them.

Dokófray met my eyes. "Progress," he said.

Danuel

Without Leonardo's interference, working with the others might go better. As I was thinking that, I turned and saw that Flistercrokta was sitting with them, doing his drill thing. I marched over, expecting to find them ready to flee from his exhaustive repetitions, but they were listening. Bonnie seemed a bit exasperated, but Sally was leaning forward, holding Lance's hand as if she were afraid he'd suddenly bolt up and run off. Matthew was sitting on the other side of Lance, not close to Bonnie, in fact, as far away as he could get. There was trouble in that relationship.

"Greetings, Flistercrokta," I said.

"You here to learn also?" he asked. I nodded and sat down. a refresher course certainly wouldn't hurt if I was going to do this with these newbies and all the ones that followed.

Only a few minutes passed before Caralee and Patsy, with Leonardo following, joined us.

"Where's Miguel?" I whispered.

"Speeta put him down for a nap. She's going to watch over him. She told me I should come here and accept more of Flistercrokta's teachings."

With the pressure removed from my shoulders, the familiar lines of Flistercrokta's wisdom began to make more sense.

"Atmosphere signifies. Assessment must be started from the beginning, but quiet is essential. Never abuse the importance of time."

Bonnie had been rolling her eyes, but at that point, it seemed that her ability to sit still and listen flew out the window. "That is the stupidest commentary I've ever heard," she said.

"It wasn't commentary," Matthew stated. "It was our doctrine, the lessons we must learn."

Bonnie huffed, then yawned at him, full-mouthed and with rude and loud ahhh's.

Matthew shook his head and said, "Sometimes, Flistercrokta, humans need to grow up before they can heed such lessons."

"I'm the same age as you, Matthew, so don't be so high and mighty."

Flistercrokta flared red eyes only a moment, then continued. "Voice gently modulated, firm. Polite. Do not engage in dialogue without the convention of civility."

That did it for Bonnie. She bolted up then ran off. Matthew started to get up to follow her, but Danuel stopped him. "Let her cool down. It is difficult to change. All this is new. Caralee and I both rebelled at first. We fought every restriction. Little Lissie threw bananas at it."

Everyone smiled then, remembering the story we'd told about three-year-old Lissie. Even Flistercrokta.

Chapter Seven

Bonnie

Everything is bad. I don't want Matthew. I want . . . well, Danuel, but that's obviously not happening. He prefers the pregnant one. Geez, I'm much prettier than her. What does Danuel see in her? But if I can't have Danuel, then I should get Leonardo. He's obviously much cooler than Matthew. Matthew is too serious, too level-headed. I want someone with some wildness in him. Okay, Danuel doesn't have that. He's all married and adult. Too adult for me, actually.

But Leonardo. He, I could go for. Except, just because Danuel and Caralee told us that Burska, a planet, for Vagabond's sake, said I'm supposed to be paired with Matthew, and Patsy gets Leonardo, it's all locked into place. I get no say in the matter. Grrr.

I bet Matthew's idea of a good time is reading a book. He'd never climb up the hill and make out on a three-moon night. That's supposed to be the most romantic of all times of the year. Mr. Swagman, Lord Tramp, and Lady Hobo all shining down, making moon shadows. It gives me goosebumps. But not if Matthew is sitting next to me.

I saw Patsy ignoring Leonardo, but when he wasn't looking, she was giving him the look. She's hooked. I think he likes her, too, because he's been following her around like the old vids of puppy dogs. I wonder what he's thinking. Does he know that this is permanent? I mean no do-overs. Whoever he picks, that's it. Final. Done.

But Matthew said that's already happened. The funny-looking herd spider, Dokófray — Danuel calls him an alien, but he looks like a herd spider to me. Except he talks and does stuff like popping in and out. Does he go invisible, or does he really jump up on some mysterious alien spaceship that we can't even see from here?

This whole thing sounds like a pot of fairy dust. It's all make-believe stuff, like herd spiders being bodyguards and growling at us. Herd spiders never did that before. My father had one. It carried him from our house to his work at the bakery. Bobo was his name, and Bobo was as dumb as a soccer ball. He never came when I called. He turned his back when he saw me coming. Just because one time I put pepper on his handful of dried insects. It wasn't that funny, either. He took one bite and spit it out all over my clean shirt.

I thought Matthew would come after me and try to get me to return to the others, to more lecturing by that even stranger herd spider, the one with the super long name that started with Flister. But no, Matthew. I guess he preferred the company of the others. Besides, he and I had yelled at each other a lot. Well, mainly, I'd done so, but he deserved it. He kept telling me that I had to adapt to things. Adapt, me? I was running back to civilization first chance I got, probably with Leonardo.

I climbed down into the sand area. That's where Lissie, Caralee's little sister, used to play. I saw the remnants of her sand castles. There'd apparently been no rain since she left. I didn't have any siblings, but if I had one, I'd be really sad if she had to leave with her parents. Planet Butterfly sounded like a nice place to go, though.

I sat down in the sand and started messing with a drawbridge. For a four-year-old, the kid had been really artistic. I probably couldn't make a castle as good as hers. I saw a wall that had crumbled a bit. I repaired it for her, just in case she came back. But that was kind of silly. I guess she wouldn't be skipping down to this area from some faraway planet. I guess that's where my parents were, Planet Butterfly. They went off without even a goodbye. But Caralee had said they were all in stasis like we'd been, so I guess they had no choice about it.

It was kind of upsetting to think about never seeing them again. They weren't the coolest, but they were my parents, and now they're gone. No more arguments. That was a plus. But on the downside, Mom used to be nice to me, buying me pretty outfits and helping me with my math. Dad was always too busy. I wouldn't miss him, but I'd miss all the cookies and breads he made.

Of course, I couldn't eat them since I knew they'd make me fat. Boys didn't like fat girls. The computer had paired me with another boy. He was going to marry me this year, but not anymore. I wondered if he was still in stasis. I guessed so. Would he be mad because I was forced to be with someone else?

In my room back at our house, I had lots of pretty things. A fancy bed, my own tele, books, and a couple of dolls from way back when. I had make-up, too, and pretty clothes. Caralee said we'd never get to return to our houses. She had tried. I bet I could sneak back in. I'd need to when my clothes got dirty. I wasn't wearing spiderwebs and leaves like Caralee. They were ugly.

It was nice down here in the sand. I could understand why Lissie used to spend her days here. I lay down in a patch lacking any castles, moats, or walls and closed my eyes to think about things. Something was blowing bubbles. At least, that's what it sounded like. I raised my head to look and almost screamed. It was a monster. A dragon monster.

I backed away slowly, watching it. It wasn't advancing on me. It was standing in the river, just staring at me.

"What do you want?" I asked.

It tilted its head. "Lissie?

My mouth fell lower, a bad habit, a very ugly habit. I slammed my lips closed. "Lissie is gone. She went to another planet."

"Oh," the dragony thing said. "When is she coming back?"

"Nobody knows. A long time from now."

"Oh," the thing said again. "Who are you? Do you like sand castles?"

This was ridiculous. I was eighteen years old. I didn't play in the sand, but I didn't think insulting a ten-foot-tall dragon was very smart. "This is my first time," I admitted.

"Oh. I taught Lissie how to make good castles. Do you want me to teach you?"

The secret of her success. I understood then why the castles looked so amazing. But why would a dragon know anything about sand castles?

"My name is Bonnie," I told him. "You don't eat people, right?"

"Of course not. Burska would never permit such things. I eat reeds and mosses. They are yummy." He started to sink back into the river but stopped. He swung back around, looked me up and down, and said, "You are pretty. But much bigger than Lissie. She was small. Oh, and my name is Claro. I am a river dragon. There are only a few of us left. Most have gone to the other side of the planet. I don't know why. That makes me lonely. Will you play with me?"

I smiled. This was absolutely crazy. No one had mentioned river dragons. Maybe Lissie had kept it a secret. Anyway, I liked Claro better than the group I was supposed to be hanging out with. "Sure," I said. "How do we start?"

It must have been hours later when Caralee came down to talk with me. I was glad it was her. I felt kind of like an extension of Lissie, and I bet she was lonely for her sister. Maybe she and I could actually be friends.

She was smiling when she saw me working in the sand. She sat down beside me and asked if she could help. I agreed, and we worked in silence for a while. But I wasn't that good at not talking, so I asked her if Lissie had ever mentioned a river dragon. Caralee stopped pushing sand against a wall and sat up, staring at me. "How did you know? She was always talking about the dragon. She even named him."

"Let me guess, Claro?"

It looked like I wasn't the only one with the jaw-dropping, amazed look. Caralee did the same thing. She stared at me, her eyes huge. "How did you know that?"

"Claro visited. He told me he used to help Lissie with her sandcastles. He helped me make this new one. Pretty cool, right?"

"You really mean it, right?" She examined me a moment. I could see the giant herd spider guarding her. He never stopped watching me, distrustfully, I imagined.

"I swear on Lady Hobo," I said. It was the old stand-by for girls. Since all the other moons had been given male names, we females had taken Lady Hobo as our patron moon. We swore on her, prayed to her, if so inclined, took our problems to her, and trusted her to be impartial with her advice. She probably was, but she'd never answered me. Some girls said that she talked to them in dreams. Anything was possible.

"Okay, you've got to tell me all about him. What's he like? Were you scared? Did he try to steal you away? No, he wouldn't have done that. He never did with Lissie. But tell me everything."

I guess I hadn't really looked at Caralee. I'd seen her as someone old, having a baby already and another on the way. But the truth was exactly what Danuel had said. Caralee was YOUNG. Her eyes were all lit up like I'd just offered her a painted icing cookie. She was babbling like the nine-year-old girl I used to sit for as our school requirement. Wow.

I told her everything I could remember, and then we talked and talked. Don't ask me about what. I couldn't remember, but we blabbed for at least an hour. Then Danuel came for her, worry tightening up his cheekbones until I swear he looked just like one of those male models who showed up now and then on vid programs, advertising men's underwear or aftershave. Of course, males no longer grew facial hair, so that was always an ad that totally fractured our funny bones, but the models left my friends and me rather Google-eyed.

"Why are you still here?" Danuel asked, sounding rather irritated. Actually, it sounded like my parents when I got home late.

Caralee didn't treat him like a parent, though. She stood up, walked toward him and, threw her arms around his neck, then kissed him a major big one. When the two of them came up for air, Caralee answered finally, "Just talking."

I was glad she told him that because prior to that, before the kiss, his eyes had stared at me with a huge hunk of rage. I think he thought I'd overpowered his wife and tied her up or something.

But Caralee wasn't done. She babbled all about the river dragon and how the thing had come up to talk with me. "He helped Bonnie with her castle. That's why Lissie always constructed them so well. She had help."

Danuel took it well. He listened, smiled, and didn't interrupt until she was finished telling him everything; then he said, "Really?"

He glanced at me. "You two pulling my leg?"

Geez, I hadn't heard that expression from anyone but my dad. It almost made me teary-eyed until I remembered that my dad and I hadn't gotten along for a very, very long time. No tears for him and not one iota of sadness. He didn't deserve it.

I backed Caralee up, then added that I'd known the dragon's name before Caralee mentioned it. Danuel shot a glance at Caralee, confirming that fact, then shifted to stare at me again.

"Okay. So you stayed down here talking with a seemingly friendly dragon while the rest of us were up there worrying about you?"

I shrugged. I wasn't going to take responsibility for that. Besides it wasn't like any of them cared what happened to me. I was the outsider of the group, the one who didn't fit well.

Caralee let go of Danuel and returned to my side. "Come on, Bonnie. You and I are going to be good friends. I'm so glad. I've been enormously lonely without my sister. Danuel's great, but you know, guys aren't a replacement for girlfriends.

I think Danuel laughed, but I was too busy searching her face for truth. She meant it. She honestly meant it!

Dokófray

Turndaloff had come down to observe. He and I had watched the entire exchange between the kids, with Flistercrokta giving lessons and then afterward. It was impressive. It was not as if Caralee and Danuel were following our lessons, but it seemed that they had their own way of going about things, one that seemed to be working.

Already, the two most troublesome of the group, Leonardo and Bonnie, were settling down. Leonardo because of Patsy, who was definitely the right choice for him, and now Bonnie because Caralee and she had bonded. I was well pleased.

I told Turndaloff that Danuel had also formed a connection with Koosk, and Caralee was letting go of Miguel, allowing Speeta to take some of the burden. It had been a good day.

Even Turndaloff, the sour sucker of the Burskans, had to agree that Burska would be content.

Matthew

They told me to let her go, but I've been worried since she left. She's to be my wife. I'm supposed to worry. I had another picked by the Mate List computer. I was resigned to that; I watched her from afar. It would have been another year until I started courting her, but I was ready. No indecision. My motto is if it's to be, then let it begin.

Several hours passed, and finally, Caralee decided to go check on her. I was very relieved. I mean, there's nothing here on Beatnik, I mean Burska, that could hurt her. No predators. But there are other dangers like falls or drowning and stuff. She'd been gone too long to still be sulking. What if she'd decided to head back to the city? I knew she and Leonardo had talked about it. Danuel had said that it wouldn't work. He'd told us all about the wall the aliens put up to keep them from returning to Caralee's farmhouse.

But I doubted that Bonnie believed that. She was kind of an *I have to see it to believe it* person. I knew I should be disappointed in the choice the aliens or Burska gave me, but I wasn't. I was frankly captivated by her wildness and her willingness to fight. It was so unlike me. I was a toe-liner. That's what my mother used to call it. One who couldn't color outside the lines or walk on the wild side. That was exactly why Bonnie had called me a dead zone. No action. No excitement.

Well, okay. But as a husband, wasn't someone with dependability what was desired? I'd be reliable. I was a good worker. She'd . . . who was I kidding? She was right. I'd never be what she wanted.

Caralee and Bonnie were walking back together, and I do mean together, like friends. I thought that Caralee would be the last person Bonnie would ever care to befriend. But there they were, whispering into each other's ears like best friends.

I looked to see what the others thought of this new change, but Sally and Lance were kissing, and Patsy and Leonardo looked to be having a very serious conversation. So, I was the odd man out. No girl for me. I'd be back to my book reading, except I had an awful feeling that there were no books here.

I was sitting over in the corner, alone as usual, when Bonnie wandered over. "I'm sorry, Matthew," she said. "I've been a real chestnut."

I had no idea what a chestnut was. Was it something good or something bad? I nodded anyway. It really didn't matter. I was just glad she was back, okay, and . . . saying she was sorry?

"It's probably my fault, Bonnie," I said. "You were right about me being a dead zone."

"No, you're not," she said, sticking her hand in mine. "I was just upset over losing my parents... . well, my mom, anyway. And then they hauled us out here in Nowhere Land, and it was just all too much. You know?"

I thought about that for a minute. We'd all lost our folks. Not even a goodbye. I had a sister who was probably still in stasis. I didn't know about the others. Were they missing relatives? Were they pining for things that would no longer be part of their lives?

"I'm sorry, Bonnie. I know this is hard. I guess we need to lean on each other."

Was that too cheezy? Did it sound like I was urging her to be closer physically? I wasn't proficient at this wooing thing. If we'd had grades like in the subjects, I probably would have failed.

"I gotta tell you what I was doing down there. You're not going to believe this," she said, and she leaned into me and started talking in a steady stream. I took it all in, gasping at the dragon part, but otherwise just hearing her out. I was hoping she'd talk all night because I was happier than a coon dog, whatever that was — another saying of my mom's. Now, I'd never get to ask her what it meant, but at the moment, I didn't care. Bonnie's sweet fragrance was washing over me, and the feel of her warm body pressed up against me was making me want to wiggle a tail like a dog on one of our old-time Earth videos.

Patsy

Leonardo certainly wasn't my first choice among the boys, but he was opening up to me more. He told me how he had wanted to be a spaceship pilot at one time, but his father said he couldn't since no one was leaving Beatnik anymore. "Kind of funny, right? He was so wrong. But anyway, after that, I thought I'd become a medical person, like a nurse or something. Only that isn't happening. Obviously. What about you?"

"A teacher. I wanted to teach the little ones, like seven or eight-year-olds."

"You can still do that," he said with enthusiasm, only he didn't get it. No books, no schools, no training programs.

"You already know what you need to know. You can teach kids to read with a stick and dirt. You can teach them to write or do math the same way. You can still be a teacher, Patsy, only it will have to be like long ago."

"But there's no kids. Well, other than baby Miguel."

"There will be. Danuel said we're going to wake up the others."

"Will you help me with it, Leonardo?" I was only asking because he seemed to have all the answers, but he took it seriously, thought about it, then said. "I would love to."

So we conversed about schools and favorite subjects then sports and hobbies. It was great. I felt like I was getting to know the real Leonardo, not the show-off, immature and sarcastic rebel.

Leonardo

Wow. I really like Patsy. She's real. Nothing fake about her. I relaxed into her, not feeling like I had to keep up a charade to be cool. She was just so easy to talk with. And her eyes, let me just say, that she's got eyes that a poet could write about. When I stare into them, I really wish I could do that kind of thing. But I'd just sound stupid. Maybe I could work with the kids on writing poems. Not about Patsy's eyes, of course, but about herd spiders and, well, being alone and . . . missing their parents.

"You know, when we wake up the little ones, they're going to be crying. Their parents are gone. We'll have to be parents for a while."

Her eyes grew even bigger, so big they were swimming pools of emotion.

"You're right," she said, her eyes actually tearing up, like that was a thing happening right this moment.

Patsy's eye lashes were long, the tears just kind of hung on them, like jewels, sparkling. I leaned in closer and touched my lips to hers. Just a brief peck, nothing like I would have done with other girls, but I wanted this to be, well, special. I didn't want her to feel pressured, either. We had time, lots of time. Right now, it was all about connections.

She gave me the hint of a smile, then said, "I think it's time to get some dinner. Are you hungry?"

I could have said a million sarcastic things about being starved enough to eat a herd spider, but I shut my lips and thought about that brief touch of my lips on hers. Sweet.

Caralee

Dokófray was there the very next morning. I thought we'd be having another day of instruction with Flistercrokta, but Burska had said we were to ride the herd of spiders to the orchard.

Miguel turned on his song and gathered the herd spiders to us. The newbies watched, eyes wide as Kiginoa bulbs. It was a sight to see this little baby, still held in my arms, crooning to wild herd spiders, some almost as big as Koosk. When they all surrounded us, their heads bowed, they collapsed themselves and waited for directions.

"Wow," said Bonnie. "How did you get the baby to do that?"

Danuel and I laughed and shrugged. There were lots of things in Burska that lacked explanations. It was better to let them flow. As Danuel had told me, "You can't swim the rapids. You just have to float." Not that I'd ever get close enough to white water to test out his theory.

When the spiders were assembled, Koosk chose riders. When everyone but Danuel and I were mounted up, I thought that meant that I'd be riding Speeta, but Dokófray ordered me to stay behind.

"Why?" So much for letting life float me down that river without fighting it. I felt full of argument. The only excitement in our lives, and I get left behind?

"In stasis or willingness," Dokófray said. I glared at him, then at Danuel.

Danuel's face showed that he didn't like that scenario either. Then I will stay behind, too," he said.

"You needed. Caralee's safety is not at risk *here*. She must protect Alexandro and Miguel."

We could feel the eyes of everyone on us, and we knew that it did little good to argue with Dokófray, but it seemed so unfair.

Danuel kissed me soundly, then said, "Speeta and Koosk will both stay, then. I'll need another ride."

There'd be no communication without Koosk. I raised an eyebrow and shook my head. "You need him, Danuel. I'll be fine with Speeta."

But Danuel had dug in his foot and planted it in beneath boulders, apparently. When the spider parade headed out, Koosk stayed behind. I waved, then turned to work on a spiderweb suit for Miguel. At least it wasn't an overnighter. I'd be fine for a day, I told myself, wiping a tear.

Lance

The attitude of the herd spiders was fascinating. I'd read about the creatures but not really had much time to mingle with them. The strange thing is that in my reading, the text books had stated that the herd spiders were low in intelligence. But I was observing some interactions that told me otherwise. For instance, how did Danuel get his attack dog spider to remain with his wife? Didn't that mean that they understood his wishes? And how had Danuel communicated? There'd been no dialogue between them.

I'd also seen times when Danuel and Caralee seemed to talk without words. It wasn't just body language, either. The interactions were too complex. And the baby. I had no words to describe what I'd seen with him. I'd never heard a baby croon like that, and I used to work with babies at the hospital ward. That was my *volunteer* work for the school, volunteer only in the sense that we got to choose our platform of activities. I figured that tending babies in a supervised arena was better than trying to figure out the needs of a bunch of younglings on my own.

But Miguel was like no baby I'd ever seen, and precociousness didn't label it solidly. I'd seen his inspections of each of us. He looked like he was diving down deep, examining our natures, our souls even. No, that baby of theirs was too weird. He was scary.

Sally didn't think so, but then she didn't know babies like I did. She just thought he had adorable smiles and giggles. I don't mean that Sally wasn't a deep thinker. She was, but she hadn't picked up on some of the things that I'd noticed. I'd been trained to observe. Individual screenings often alerted the hospital to potential health conditions. My mind was full of checklists.

It was interesting to me the way that Dokófray separated the couple. The alien policed us all with this nonspecific protocol, ignoring things I'd have thought he'd call us on, then threatening subtle challenges. Of course, Leonardo was a handful. Maybe he did need to be returned to stasis, but he seemed better with Patsy.

The pairings, which I'd first secretly rejected, had turned out okay. Sure, I'd had another chosen for me by the Mating List, but there'd been no interaction between us. She was young, so I'd kept away. But Sally was okay. I liked her. She was a good kisser. I wondered about that. Had she and her listed guy gotten that close? Was she . . . It didn't matter. When Fate throws you a loop, the only thing to do is catch it.

My herd spider was an ugly, black, and brown. I think she was a female since they were supposed to be bigger, but with this group, Koosk was the biggest, and he was definitely a male. We were given no reins to hold, like I'd seen in video reels. No harness of any kind or saddle. We just plonked ourselves in the middle between their abdomen and their front part. The prosoma or thorax, I think I remember it being called. My spider had black or brown fuzz all over him or her, with black tripes running up the legs. I wondered if someone had named the thing.

Leonardo was making snide remarks about his spider, calling the thing a slow-moving rock. I think he was forgetting that spiders had fangs and venom. I reminded him about that, and he stopped making fun of it. I know Danuel once spoke of getting spider-bitten. He'd said it was painful.

We moseyed along, passing through woods with really excellent trees for house building. I thought maybe we could use a few for our huts that Danuel had said we were supposed to build. I'd never read any books about construction. It was good that he had some experience in doing so. I'd noticed turtle shells on the roof. I thought we weren't ever to touch them since they were protected, but this was a new universe. I guess that was up to Burska, and she'd apparently approved it. I couldn't see the advantage. They looked odd for roofing, like giant pimples atop layers of reeds and leaves.

We finally arrived at the orchard. Wow. I'd never seen so many fruits dangling from trees. Too bad they weren't the kind we were supposed to eat. Wait. I guess we had been eating them. I'd forgotten, having never seen them except in our daily allotment, handed to us individually.

I jumped down when told to. I wasn't crossing Dokófray. An alien, Danuel had said. I guessed that meant he was from some other world. Why was he here?

He made me nervous. He'd never turned his glare on me. I think I was on his okay list, but it was better to be cautious.

Sally walked up to me and took my hand. I liked that she reached out to me. It made our relationship more certain.

I noticed that the other two couples did the same thing, linking hands standing together for either safety or companionship. Meanwhile, our spiders wandered off, scooping up insects with an eagerness that was more like Miguel's greed for the fruit paste his parents shoveled into his mouth. The six of us stood in a semi-circle, waiting for directions. Those came from Danuel as he shoved spiderweb bags in our hands and told us we were supposed to collect fruits from the trees. He gave us a minute of instruction, denoting which ones would keep better vs. the ones already ripe and ready to eat.

"You should all eat one," Danuel said. "But being greedy and eating more will give you a tummy ache. I know," he said with a grin on his face that looked half grimace and half embarrassment.

So we went our separate ways in couples. Sally turned out to be a good harvester. Her legs skimmed up the tree as easily as if she were one of the monkeys in a zoo video. Of course, her legs were much more fun to look at. Good thing she was wearing jeans, or I might have lost all interest in collecting fruit.

Danuel

We worked for about an hour, I estimated. Once my bag was filled up, I started on another and then a third. I figured that was one for each member of my family, not counting Alexander, since he, obviously, couldn't eat any in his current position inside Caralee's tummy.

Then, when I was finished, I tracked down Dokófray, who was surprisingly still hanging around. He wasn't collecting fruits, so I didn't know why, but I saw that he was keeping his eye on both Leonardo and Bonnie, which couldn't have been easy to do since they had gone separate ways.

"Why did you make Caralee stay home?"

Dokófray met my eyes. *Miguel had dream. Bad dream. He say Alexandro want to come now. Too early. Caralee need to rest more. Not climb trees or take long trip to orchard near her farmhouse.*

We go soon to wake others. Young ones. Not take Caralee. Not safe. This prepare her. Long trip, Four day. You not stay with her.

Now, it made more sense. Why hadn't Dokófray told her that? But then I used my common sense. Caralee would not have listened, and she would have stressed out even more."

"In Miguel's dream, were Caralee and Alexandro okay?"

Uncertainty. Warning. We follow Burska. She say no, go. Caralee stay.

I found the information worrisome to the point that I wanted to get back to her immediately. I called everyone together and told them to mount up.

"No spiders," Leonardo said, but the moment that was noted, the spiders returned.

No tell Caralee, Dokófray warned me as we mounted up.

I nodded. I agreed that it would be better to say nothing, but it would be difficult to hide the information from her. Our minds flowed together too much.

With the bags hanging from the spiders' necks and everyone secured, I urged the herd spiders to return with more speed. Surprisingly, they seemed to hear that, for their formerly laggard pace sped up, and although we didn't gallop our return, we did do a faster pace.

The moment we rode into the what Caralee now called the village, Caralee came running outside. She had Miguel on her hip and was holding him in place to run better.

"Easy, wife," I said. "I am happy, very happy to see you, but you need to think of Alexandro. He might not like being jiggled."

She laughed, and I saw that I hadn't made my scolding sharp enough. I would need to have a talk with her, not revealing my conversation with Dokófray, but reminding her that she must go slower when pregnant.

She was probably not more than four or five months along. It shouldn't be that important to avoid strenuous activity, but with the new knowledge Dokófray had given me, I became more aware.

I kissed her contently but then pulled her back. "I'm serious, Caralee. No more running. Remember that time you fell and broke your shoulder?"

"I was a fool then. Now I'm older and wiser," she teased.

But I remained stern. "Promise me," I demanded. "No more running."

Miguel had been quiet throughout that semi-lecture. I attended to him then, pulling him into a swift hug then tickling him. When he stopped giggling, he stared into my eyes. *"Yes,"* he said. *"Mommy does not heed such things. Even Koosk cannot stop her."*

Dokófray, I sent into the void, figuring he'd gone back to his ship. *You may have to pull Caralee up to your ship like you did with Lissie that time. She will not listen to us. Miguel said so.*

Too loud, he said. *I am behind you.*

He did not respond to my request but instead addressed Caralee. *What did you do while we were gone?*

She rattled off a series of activities, but Koosk told me a truer version. *She went down to the sand and tried to interact with the river dragon. He didn't show up so she walked to the tree for fresh Gorla fruit. She was going to climb the tree, but I stopped her. I picked fruit for her. She was very angry.*

Tell Dokófray I sent, feeling guilty because I was in a sense snitching, and even worse, perhaps, using Koosk to spy on her.

We sat down a few minutes later in the place we'd named our campfire circle, even though we never set a fire. But it was a good place for discussions and lessons, so we'd adapted it for more comfortable seating, the guys having hauled logs so everyone had a backrest.

I led us off, saying, "The fruit you collected will be yours, but remember, eat only one per meal, no more than two each day. Discarded turtle shells, for some reason, seem to keep the fruit from over-ripening, so it should be good for a week or more. We also use the shells for face and hand washing. We have extras or you can scout out your own. I recommend doing some hiking to explore your area more thoroughly. I haven't really checked it out for resources like the shells. If you find another quiet beach, let everyone know. That would benefit us all. But feel free to bathe in the beach area anytime you want, but of course, the river, even here, is too fast moving for swimming. But its water is drinkable.

"Dokófray has given us permission to harvest some trees for construction, so we will start that tomorrow morning. Unfortunately, you'll need to make your own cutting tools. I chipped rock for a good edge, but even so, handmade axes are not quality tools. Cutting down even one tree is laborious. We will work together on it. Women, if you want to go with us or not. But if you choose to participate, you must have your own tool.

"I will try not to be chauvinistic in such things, but, as you know, Burska has given males some nice muscles that she didn't give you as generously, so . . . Did I say that un-chauvinistic enough, my darling?"

Caralee laughed, then skipped her gaze about the female part of the group. She nodded.

"We girls might like to take the opportunity to bathe without males oogling us," she said, laughing a bit nervously.

I saw three eager nods from the girls. I wondered if I should warn them about what Dokófray had done to us, but I let it go. He would probably not appreciate my interference if he had similar plans for these newbies.

Caralee

A few days later, I had a vivid Miguel dream. The herd spiders had lined up for our departure to the stasis huts. Dokófray was telling me that, again, I could not go, and I was ranting about it. Instead of arguing, Dokófray sent me up to the ship, where I had to stay in that same small room where we'd had our mentoring lessons. Only this time, there was no Danuel or Lissie with me. I was alone with nothing to do, no one to talk to, and not even baby Miguel, who'd stayed in our village with Speeta.

It was a horrible dream. I woke up sobbing. I poured out the horror of it to Danuel, and he got very quiet,

"I won't get to go to the stasis huts with you, will I?" I asked.

"I'm sorry, sweetheart. Burska's orders."

"And Miguel was warning me what would happen if I didn't accept it?"

Both Miguel and Danuel met my eyes. Neither said anything. Of course, Miguel still wasn't talking, but he had his ways of communicating when he wanted to. And Danuel was merely looking sad-eyed.

"Okay," I said. "No running. No climbing trees. Koosk will be in charge of me. I've been regressed to Lissie-age, right?"

Okay, so I was handing out a massive guilt trip, as my parents used to call it, but geez. I was pregnant, not sick. And shouldn't I be allowed to monitor my own health?

I got up out of bed, not even nursing Miguel. No, I wasn't angry at the baby, but I did need to visit the bushes, and in the dream, he'd been just fine with Speeta. Maybe it wasn't their fault for curbing my wing feathers, but it still hurt.

Outside, I ran into Sally. She was jogging by. I waved a hello while I was washing my hands, and she ran over to chat. "You know what I found out about Lance? He worked in the hospital with the babies. Any questions you might have, he could . . . Oh, sorry. I wasn't thinking. Of course, you've already been through this once. You probably know more than all the rest of us combined. In fact, when I get pregnant, I'll be coming to you to ask my questions."

I recognized the babble zone. We all used it when we made a gaffe. I'd babbled sometimes just from nerves.

"That's good to know, Sally. I appreciate your telling me that. I guess we're going to help each other in everything in the future. Right?"

She nodded, then motioned further ahead. "I need to jog on. I've got to get my heart rate up. See you."

That was like a slap in the face, an unintentional slap. But it hurt just the same. That used to be me jogging at the side of my father. We ran almost every single day, except the sixth day off when we only speed walked. Now, I was deeply out of shape and probably couldn't run a block. I'd promised Danuel no running, but the moment Alexandro was born, I was getting back into daily exercise. Maybe Sally and I could run together once I got back in shape.

When I returned to the hut, a hungry Miguel was waiting. Danuel had been feeding him fruit paste, but the baby wanted me. I sat down on the bed and let him nurse. I thought about asking Lance how long I needed to continue nursing, but that would be embarrassing. Maybe I could ask Sally, and she could find out.

"Nursing is good for the baby," Danuel said, jumping in on my private thoughts.

"Then why don't you do it?" I said angrily.

Miguel stopped and looked up at me. His eyes studied me. I knew he was reading me. I could tell now. His eyes turned darker, almost black, when he did that.

"Never mind, Miguel. Mommy's just cranky this morning. I saw Sally jogging and missed it. I used to be in top condition, and now I'm not even healthy enough to ride a herd spider."

Danuel threw an arm around me and pulled me closer, but it was so gently done that Miguel, who'd gone back to his nursing, didn't disengage.

"Look, Burska wanted her spider hopper and her judge. Maybe she'll give us some slack after that and let us have the freedom to jog and goof around."

"Five kids," I said. "Burska is relentless."

"Yeah, but that doesn't mean all at once. Maybe we'll have twins. Maybe . . ."

Miguel chose that moment to send the newest image. Carolina was cute as could be. She looked a little like Lissie, same hair and eye color, but not with Lissie's stubborn chin. Then came Angelica and Fernando, both almost carbon copies of Danuel. But no twins. Five separate births.

"Okay," Danuel said. "If Burska's going to be that demanding, then I'll carry the last two in my belly."

"Yeah, right," I said.

By then, I was giggling, and Danuel was getting frisky. Who knows what might have happened if Koosk hadn't entered the hut and let Danuel know that the others were waiting for him?

"Vagabond, I forgot," Danuel said, springing up, then doubling back to kiss my cheek. "See you later. I love you, sweetheart."

Lady Hobo, I'd been such a grouch. Danuel was the sweetest man in the world, and he had to put up with my grumbling.

Miguel stopped nursing to smile up at me. Then he yawned. He had another tooth breaking free of the gum. Poor guy. Mommy feeling sorry for herself, and he was probably in pain.

I hugged him to me, then burped him. He wiggled free, wanting down on the ground. The floor of our hut had sand on it, so it was soft for crawling, but Miguel found it harder to pull himself up. He raised up his arms and cried, "Mama, mama, walk."

There was no way he was talking yet, but the sound of his demand was clear. I knew just what he wanted. I picked him up and carried him outside, plopping him down in the area where the new logs had been placed for back rests. That was Miguel's favorite place. I think he thought the logs had been arranged for him.

"You're too young to be walking," I told him.

"My mom always said it was pure gumption that made a kid walk," Patsy said. "Miguel has that in spades."

He may have wanted to practice standing and walking, but the approach of the girls changed his mind. He put out his arms and said, "Patsy."

The other two came up a moment later, having heard Miguel's clarity. "What's my name?" Bonnie asked him.

"Bonn," he said.

"And me?" Sally asked.

"Shally,"

"Wow. You are one smart cookie," Sally said. "You wanna go swimming, Miguel?"

He nodded, but that sent him tumbling back into the dirt. "May I?" Sally asked.

I nodded and was delighted to feel no green jealousy demon gnawing at my insides.

We walked down to the beach where Lissie used to play, and I almost didn't feel the pang of missing her. Miguel was laughing, and the girls were teasing him. Alexandro was kicking my insides. It was a good day.

Dokófray

All good. Burska happy but says time to get young ones. The six take, two each couple. I agree, but watch Caralee. She worries me. Miguel say, not resting.

Miguel calls the herd spiders. We prepare to go. Caralee does not argue. But Bonnie speaks up. She wants to stay with Caralee. Twelve children in stasis. Five plus Danuel. Two each. Yes, can do. I wait for Danuel. He decide.

"Caralee, do you want that? Is that a good idea?" Danuel asked.

"Please, Danuel. Please let her stay. I won't be as lonely then. You can take Koosk, and . . ."

"No. Koosk remains," he said.

I agreed with decision. Koosk guards Miguel and Caralee. Speeta still not able. Soon spider sac hung, but not yet.

"Okay," Caralee said in a little girl voice.

I smiled. She sounded like Lissie.

Matthew

Bonnie talked to me about her decision to stay. I couldn't say no. I didn't own her, but I really didn't want to see her stay behind. We hadn't been together long. In fact, we'd only just started talking. Even so, if she was supposed to become my wife, shouldn't I feel betrayed that she didn't want to come with us? Well, not betrayed exactly. Only shouldn't she want to be with me? Maybe she needed time out to be away from me for a while.

None of the guys had moved in on the girls. The girls all slept next to each other; *a sleepover every night* is how Sally put it. We guys stayed near them like we needed to protect them or something, but I think the girls would have preferred a bit more distance. But who knew? I couldn't read them well. I had no idea what Bonnie was thinking most of the time.

Caralee was easy to read. She had that kind of face that showed every thought. She blushed, too. I found that enchanting. Not that I was panting over Danuel's wife. I didn't mean that at all. It was just that I could use some *simple to read* with Bonnie.

Danuel was lucky. I'd admit that. He knew what he was doing. That's the main thing. I wondered how he'd achieved that. Was it being older or just having known her longer?

I bet Danuel was missing his wife. They seemed really close.

Maybe I could talk with him. He seemed like a good guy. I liked that he worked hard and didn't show off. He knew lots about living in the wild, too, and I had a lot of questions to ask.

But how did one push a spider forward? What was the key to guiding the thing? Perhaps that would be my first question if I ever figured out how to move up beside Danuel. Except, when I looked to see where he was, I saw that, for some reason, Dokófray was riding a spider beside Danuel's. I thought the alien had his own way of getting places, using some kind of magical tech thing.

The two kept talking for a long time. Then, suddenly, the alien's spider was walking alongside Danuel with no rider on his back. Strange. But it did give me an idea. I climbed down from my beast and walked toward Danuel.

"Hey, is it okay if I ride beside you? I'd like to get to know you and ask some questions."

Danuel looked unsure about that, but he didn't say no. I didn't know which part he wasn't okay with, but I assumed he'd agreed, so I started to climb the spider's leg. That didn't work well. The spider shook his leg and threw me off.

"Whoops." I tried again, then again.

Finally, Danuel called a halt. Somehow, although I didn't see him gesture and I know he didn't say anything, all the spiders stopped.

"The secret to herd spiders, I think, is to talk to them," Danuel said. "Ask the spider if you can ride. Address a spider with formality and graciousness. Address one like you know that the spider's your equal in status."

Maybe I didn't want to be friendly with the guy. He sometimes talked super crazy, but I thought it was worth trying his way. He did seem to have an in with the spiders.

"What's his name?" I asked.

"She. The spider is female. I don't know her name. You'll have to ask her."

Okay, now the guy believed that the herd spiders could talk. How did Caralee put up with him?

The herd spider looked down at me with those two black eyes the herd spiders have, the big ones. I knew they also had six more that were used for other things.

"I'm Leonardo," I said, a friend of Danuel and Caralee."

I felt a tickle in my forehead and scratched it, but nothing else. No other reaction from the huge beast.

"Is it all right to climb up?" I asked Danuel.

"You can try it. I can't speak to her. Only Koosk."

I stroked her side, then set a foot on her leg. She didn't shake it this time. I lifted myself up, half-cliff, half-pole climbing, but I reached the top.

"Thank you, ma'am. What is your name?"

I wished I could hear something, but she remained silent. But the important thing is that I'd achieved a seat on her. That was worth a cheer, except we'd been lectured by Flister about not being loud, so I sucked it in and glanced over at Danuel.

"What do you mean that you can speak to Koosk? Like he obeys voice commands?"

Danuel laughed. "You really don't understand herd spiders if you think that. First off, toss out everything they taught you in school. Herd spiders are smart. They understand our language. Sometimes, they're willing to communicate with us, but mostly not. It took almost a year before Koosk decided to speak with me. He and I didn't always have a great relationship. Not after he bit me."

"Yeah, I don't understand that. At school, they said . . . Yeah, forget that. But I thought they never bit people because we taste bad."

"We probably taste better after we've been living on Burska's fruit and roots, but that's not the key part. They don't have a reason to bite . . unless you give them one."

"Okay, I get it. But they're bigger than us. Why do they hang around and give us rides when we want to go someplace?"

"I think Burska told them to, but other than that, I don't know. Lots of stuff happens on the planet that I haven't figured out. I never know what Dokófray is going to tell us to do. Or why. Or when. He does what Burska tells him to do. He's told me that, but why? That I don't know either. He and the other aliens live in a spaceship. Why do they care what a planet wants them to do? If you ask Dokófray such things, he'll just walk away. He rarely explains anything."

I nodded, taking it in. Danuel was right; the whole thing with aliens and talking planets was a brain-twisting weirdness. But this was my chance to learn what he did know, so I plowed on.

"Something else I've been thinking about, Danuel. Bonnie or one of the other girls said that you and Caralee were on the Mate List together. But the rest of us weren't. We were assigned to others. Why do you think Burska paired you two? Why didn't she pick our Mate List partner to wake us up with? Not that I'm complaining. I think Bonnie is great."

Danuel was constantly scanning the way ahead, the woods on both sides of us, and looking back to make sure everything was okay. What did he expect would happen when there weren't any predators or awakened humans beside us? Danuel's eyes returned to me, and I could see he was thinking about my question. His eyes went fuzzy. I could almost see brain cells whirling.

"Caralee and I were already pretty tied together, I guess. Besides, since we were a unit, maybe it was just easier for Burska. The planet didn't have to do whatever she does to assess who each of us would best partner with. I'm glad that was the route she took because I was already in love with Caralee by the time the aliens captured us. I'd never have gone along with being matched with someone else. Or at least I wouldn't have wanted to."

"And Caralee, was she already in love with you?"

Danuel shook his head and laughed. "No, she was scared to death of me. The List announcement, for those who'd turned fifteen that year, was read out loud at school. She'd just turned fifteen the day before and wasn't ready for that particular assembly. Hearing my name as her future mate scared her away from the friendship I was establishing. After that, she wouldn't let me get closer than four feet before she took off running."

"So you were already courting her?" I asked, surprised because that wasn't supposed to be allowed, not when one partner was still only fifteen. Most families required the traditional eighteen years for linkage. That was why none of us had started courtship with our mates yet.

"No. Her parents never would have permitted an early engagement. But they were agreeable to the mate pairing. They'd even offered to bring me into their herd spider training program. But that would have been a few years later. No, I was just trying to become her friend then, to get her to know me better.

"I was working for the grocery store, delivering groceries. Remember the orchard where we harvested the fruit? Her parents' farmhouse was about a half mile further on. She was there all alone, as I told you guys, babysitting her three-year-old sister the day the aliens came. I'd just arrived with her food delivery. Pure chance I was there. A lucky chance since Burska might have paired her with someone else if I hadn't been on the scene."

"Yes, I remember the spider webbing of the girls and how you were shot with stasis. That must have been terrifying. So only you three were taken up into the alien ship? Why did they pick you?"

Danuel's eyes were scanning again, looking for . . . what? Was he just the nervous sort, assuring himself that there weren't any spiderwebs waiting to capture us? Or did he know something we didn't about the dangers in the woods? I wanted to ask him, but I wasn't finished with this subject yet.

Apparently, we were currently safe from wild beasts and stray aliens. He returned to my question. I liked that the guy seemed a straight shooter, as my pops used to say, meaning Danuel didn't hold back. He answered each question with directness and an openness that surprised me. He seemed as honest as a video lie detector.

"I don't know why we were the ones they picked for their version of enlightenment. Dokófray said there were other teens who ran into the woods to hide. But those kids either died or failed. I never got a solid answer about what went wrong or what their fate was. I do know that the ones who failed and lived were sent up in the ship with their parents. None of them are in stasis. At least, that's what I was told.

"But, as far as I know, Caralee, Lissie, and I were the only ones taken up onto the ship. Believe me, we would have been happier to let anyone else take our place. It wasn't fun *to be put in a box even with a ribbon on top.*"

I smiled at him using one of our sayings, but then I remembered that Danuel wasn't more than a year or two older than me. He just acted older because he'd been on his own so long. Plus, his body no longer appeared that of a teenager. With all his muscles and wrinkle lines in the forehead, he'd crossed the border into adulthood.

Maybe that's what being married and having kids did to you. That was something to think about, although the concept didn't seem like a bad thing. It would be worse to be stuck in middle-land where you weren't a kid, and you weren't considered mature enough to make hard decisions. And there'd be a wife involved, the gorgeous Bonnie. I wet my lips and closed my eyes a moment, picturing that.

Then I pulled myself out of my semi-sexual vision and said, "So you actually were in stasis a while, just like us, just not as long, right?"

"Right, and when they woke us up, we argued, just like you did. We fussed, we struggled, we hit and kicked. Except we were deprived of food, water, and a toilet for days, and most of those days, we thought the aliens were going to eat us.

"At least you six lucked out in that way. You got food, water, and freedom, well, limited freedom, but we were cramped up in a single room, which was our biggest blessing and our biggest fear because we were constantly worried that the aliens would separate us again."

Wow. This guy had a Mr. Swagman kind of story, although why a moon would have a story, I'd never figured out, but that was the expression. I thought about what that must have been like and decided that he was right. Our version of alien capture was a lot better than his.

We kept riding for another hour or so, the two of us tossing the conversation ball back and forth. Then we stopped to rest and eat a fruit. Then, more travel and unending boredom, or so it seemed.

When we finally halted for the night to bed down, I went back to the others. I needed to reconnect and tell them what I'd learned. It was probable that they hadn't missed me. They were sitting closely, each paired with their new mate. I felt like the odd one out, even though it was just temporary. But it suddenly struck me how much I missed Bonnie. It was like losing a leg. Nah, that's too icky. Like being alone. That's what it was. Solitary when I'd been starting to becoming entwined.

I grabbed the blanket from my pack, the spiderweb one that Caralee had made for each of us. The blanket felt cold at first, but it warmed up with my body heat. Not that the air was cold or anything. The planet used to be ice cold and damp at night, but not anymore. We could now be fairly comfortable even without a blanket, but I liked having a cover. More protection than warmth, I supposed.

Caralee had once mentioned that the planet was trying to accommodate to our needs. That was an interesting thought. Why would a planet care about us? What did she get out of it taking care of a bunch of humans? And why did she push the herd spiders to serve us? What was up with that?

Chapter Eight

Bonnie

Hanging out with Caralee was fun. She had a really good sense of humor and no artifice. She was simple, in a way, uncomplicated, but I liked that about her. I compared her to my former friends, the ones probably still in stasis. With them, friendship was a contest of one-upmanship. Who got so and so to flirt first, who had a new outfit, or who got the best grade on an exam?

Of course, we'd done activities together, but baking cookies wasn't much fun when we were all on a diet, and the only time we tried to hike up a trail, Sandy twisted her ankle, and we had to carry her whining self down the path. Funny how she got better when Brad saw us and came over to help. No more pain, then. No more whining either, just hair tossing and simpering over his strength and his (actually subpar) muscles that made you sick to your stomach.

Now, if Danuel had done the knight to the rescue bit for me, simpering would have been acceptable. He was a real hunk, one a girl could drool over, like those idols on the old Earth videos. But I was careful not to mention such thoughts to Caralee. It would surely end any friendship between us. Besides, it was obvious they were on lock and hold. No questions about that.

I wondered why Caralee had such low self-esteem. She was pretty in her own way. Good complexion, great hair, although she did nothing with it, leaving it tied in a low ponytail. I wondered if she'd like some tips, but I stayed clear of that. I didn't want her to see me as the interfering big sister. In a beauty contest, she'd strike out. I always came first in those, but maybe she had talent. I wondered if she could sing. She might have been a dancer, but obviously, that wasn't happening now with her current sports ball-belly attachment.

I got the feeling that she felt she'd missed out on her education. But I wasn't sure that mattered all that much here. Where would she need the skills to compare and contrast the interactions between fictional characters or label the fractions of a peach pie? Algebra wouldn't help her to fix a torn spiderweb shirt. And learning a foreign language? Real useful when we all spoke the common tongue.

I wanted to tell Caralee that she hadn't missed much, but maybe she was right. Maybe school had taught me some things I was grateful for. My favorite class had been visitations, where we'd dropped in for a week of real work experience in multiple locations. I'd done a hospital stint, a school, a bakery, a drug supply company, a farm, and been engaged in a civil government seminar.

Also, I got to shadow a high school principal as he supervised the school. That was cool, major insight in what the teacher's lounge looked like, and I learned that the teachers traded stories about us students just as much as we whispered about the teachers.

Caralee's low part seemed to come from her heavy dose of isolation. Being raised on a herd spider farm and needing to babysit nonstop had kept her from doing most of the fun stuff in the city. She'd never even gone to a school game. Not that they were the highlight of my former life. But no ice cream parlor, no amateur theatre productions, and no sleepovers with her buddies. She'd hardly lived before she was swept into the alien invasion and babymaking.

The other girls oohed and aahed over baby Miguel. He was cute, all right, but he was constantly needing a change or wanting to suck on Caralee's boobs. When he crawled over to me and pulled himself up to do his wobbly stand-up, of course, I made the required sounds of admiration, but I found such things tedious. I mean, why get excited about a kid doing something like that? Everyone eventually learned to stand up, and they didn't need to hold onto *my* jeans to do it.

Caralee's herd spider, Speeta, gave me the creeps. She was constantly watching me like she thought I was going to do something horrible to Caralee. Like what? Get her to take drugs or get drunk? That only happened in the movies. Nobody on Beatnik, I mean Burska, did those things. The most exciting thing we did was to make out with a guy who wasn't our Mate Listed guy. But few of us bothered. The consequences if we were caught were too severe.

Strangely, that was exactly what I'd been doing since stasis. Matthew and I hadn't done much more than exchange a few kisses, but those would have put us in a trouble cell and earned a call to our parents. Here, that stuff was encouraged, maybe even demanded. One of our exchanged stories had been Caralee telling me about Dokófray stealing her clothes and ordering the two of them to marry each other. Geez. Not a lot of romance in that. Danuel didn't even get to woo her with gifts and flowers.

I wondered if Matthew would court me. We were stuck with each other, and he wasn't a bad guy. I'd asked Caralee what she thought of Matthew, and she praised him a lot. She talked about his good qualities so much so, in fact, I even felt a sharp pain of jealousy. Talk about ridiculous. Me jealous of someone eyeing Matthew?

But Caralee was right. I had noticed his soft brown eyes and the way his nose looked rather aristocratic. She'd said that he was a deep thinker, the kind of person who didn't sway in the breeze but thought things out. How did she get to be so assured in her judgments, and how did she know that kind of detail about Matthew?

I asked. She blinked, then seemed to go into hiding. I wondered what that was about. Had she been messing around with my beau? But it wasn't anything like that, I wormed it out of her finally and discovered that she was empathetic. She got flashes of knowledge just from looking at people. Wow. That would save a lot of grief — like when the one you just told your secrets to turned out to be a real jerk, blabbing it to everyone who'd listen.

So she could ascertain character with a glance. "So, why did you allow me to stay with you?" I asked, meaning it but turning it into a light-hearted flippancy.

She stared into my eyes, searching for mockery but finding none, smiled, then shrugged. "I didn't like you when you were hanging out with Leonardo. The two of you together brings out the worst in each of you, but now that you and Matthew are forming a relationship, you're different. You've relaxed into who you are supposed to be, a caring and very likeable person.

At home, my parents used to play a very, very old Earth series called the Twilight Zone. It began each segment with its own spooky-themed music. I was playing it in my ear right then. Caralee was deep. It's not simple at all. She was someone I'd esteem to have like me, to become a really good friend.

She laughed when I told her that, and then the same low self-esteem problem reared its ugly head. "Why would you want me as your friend? I'm backward, ignorant, and . . ."

"Wow. Stop right there. I don't think a single one of us would call you that. And Burska would never have chosen you for your position if you weren't someone very, very special."

"Maybe she chose me because I can bear children for her. A good broodmare, they used to call it in horse movies."

Koosk had just entered the hut to hear that. He growled low, his huge beady eyes fastened on Caralee.

"Someone's in trouble," I whispered, not at all sure I was kidding.

She glanced up at Koosk. "Yeah, I know, Koosk. I'm supposed to be honored by the tribute of giving birth to the spider hopper and the judge, but being pregnant isn't fun, and I think I'm really tired of it, but Burska plans to make me have five children. I'm furious about that. Why can't Bonnie, Patsy, or Sally carry the next babies? Why does it have to be me?"

I thought she was just letting off steam, but Koosk walked closer, lowered his head into her lap, then stared into her eyes like he was trying to tell her something.

As if he'd succeeded, he backed away, and then Caralee started sobbing.

Leonardo

I thought Matthew had a good idea in getting to know Danuel better. That could be considered, according to one of my school classes, net-working, which was a good method for attaining political supporters and in social ladder climbing. But what was the point here? Danuel had the chief position. There wasn't any changing that. I dallied with the idea for a moment but decided to encourage Lance. I'd rather stay near Patsy, defending the romantic positioning I'd achieved with her so far.

Lance accessed me, attempting to figure out my reasoning. I knew he didn't trust me. He was rather a skeptical guy; I was learning. In fact, skeptical was putting it too mildly. He just plain didn't trust me.

I could see he was thinking it over, but he turned to Sally had asked her opinion. "Yes, let's," she said.

Wow. I should have thought of that. I could have asked Patsy to come with me and won points for being, what . . . non-chauvinistic?

"You might have a problem with the herd spider, though," I said. "Danuel made Matthew talk to the animal like it spoke our language, and he had to ask permission to ride it."

"Sally cooed. That's so adorable. Of course, we must do that. They seem lots smarter than we were told. I think Danuel's right. That Koosk is like a vid movie about a dog. He watches for danger and alerts Danuel. He seems to follow conversations, too. Maybe the herd spiders are our equal."

She stopped babbling to ponder what she'd said. Lance looked over at me and winked.

Sally came out of her speculation mode to start talking with her mount. "Hey, I'm Sally. Thank you for being willing to let me ride on top of you. I really, really appreciate it. Do you think we could head over to where Danuel is? I'd like to get to know him better. Would you mind . . .?"

Before she could finish the thought, the herd spider was galloping forward. I watched as he headed directly to the beast Danuel was riding.

"Tough luck, old chap," I told Lance. "Looks like your future wife is going to get the chance to make eyes at the head wrangler."

Lance's face turned red, almost as bad as Caralee's blushes. He kicked his beast. "Hey, Buster, let's go. I need to catch up with my girlfriend."

The herd spider turned his head in a way he shouldn't have been allowed to and stared at Lance. It was ominous. I thought Lance was a goner for sure, but then the spider turned his head back around and plugged on. I didn't see Lance do any more kicking, but he sat in hump mode for a good quarter of an hour before slinging a leg over the side of his spider and running on his own two feet to catch up with Sally.

"You're a mischief-maker," Patsy said.

"Is that a negative or a positive," I said trying to joke her out of her crossness.

"That depends on whether you expect me to bow down to Burska's wishes or not."

Ah, whether she'd be willing to become my wife? Well, I wasn't sure about that either. Girlfriend, maybe, but wife? She was a potential, let's just say.

"I see," I said. "Uh, maybe you'll be able to teach me to be a better person?"

"You better hope so because the alternative is a very dry spell for you. Permanently."

Ouch, okay, the challenge was on. Patsy was a definite. Now I had to think back concerning all those school lessons about wooing a girl. Geez, I'd slept through most of them.

Danuel

The night was tough to get through. I almost couldn't sleep without the feel of Caralee in my arms. She'd become my teddy bear, so to speak. Koosk had offered to send one of the herd spiders to wrap me up in hairy arm and arms, and I'd laughed at the time. I wondered if Caralee was doing that. Would Koosk treat her like he had Lissie?

But she had Bonnie with her, Bonnie the rebel. I wondered how that was going. I hoped Koosk would send me a message if something went wrong, but then, probably not. He'd deal with it himself. I glanced up at Lord Tram and Lady Hobo. They were playing footsie with their slightly yellow orbs, neither showing a lot of light that night. Why was I so restless? I felt like something was plaguing me, something besides the lack of Caralee.

I must have slept some because I woke up with a herd spider nuzzling me. "Okay, I'm awake," I said, brushing her gently away.

"I am Carry," she said.

"I'm Danuel," I replied courteously.

She giggled. Did herd spiders giggle? But it was a similar sound, anyway. "Everyone knows you, First Father," she said with a bow.

"Is there a message from Koosk?" I asked.

"No, but from Dokófray. He says we must go now so we can return speedily."

"Carry, is something wrong with Caralee or Miguel? Are they okay?"

"I do not know, only that we must go quickly. Then return. Burska say. Dokófray say."

I sounded the alarm for heading out, then allowed a few minutes to make sure everyone had returned from their visits to the woods, then we were marching forward in less than ten minutes, or so I estimated.

I urged a faster pace, and we arrived about the time the sun was at its zenith. The early explorers had named the sun, but I couldn't remember what they'd finally decided to call it. It was a different name than sun. I'd have to ask the others if they remembered.

But we searched through the kids, looking for the ones that Burska had selected. They were thankfully in a group, which eased our hunt significantly. Dokófray had already assigned their keepers. I was to carry Bonnie's two: Brilla and Greg. I checked in on the others. They were toting their kids out to the spiders, seemingly in an equal rush as I was. What was up with my itchy feeling, which seemed to be driving this urgent need to return as swiftly as possible?

We used the reed twine we'd braided with the harnesses Caralee had made and fastened the kids on the spare spiders. Then, once everything had been checked and rechecked, we headed out, not even stopping to rest. Everyone had fruit in their packs, so we needed no meal breaks, only stopping when someone needed the other kind of break, and that was a quick pause.

By galloping a bit and not taking rest breaks, we made it back without having to take another overnight. We marched into our river village just as dark was falling. Caralee and Bonnie appeared from the hut. Caralee and I took a moment for a deep kiss and a swift smooch for Miguel, and then I turned and urged everyone to unload the kids. Everyone was done before Sir Vagabond had taken his moment to light up the sky. With the kids like standing pretzels, as Caralee called it, I sent the six to their beds and thanked all the herd spiders.

Koosk had stood back, waiting his turn for attention. I went to him, threw my arms about his neck — okay, first time for everything — and said, "What is wrong? Carry told me to hurry back here."

The image that Koosk shot me was as clear as Miguel's always was. *A spaceship was coming; It would reach us on another day.*

Burska said it was from Earth and was carrying a great many weapons.

"What is it? Is something wrong?" Caralee cried out, pulling me back from Koosk.

So she hadn't been told. Burska was still worried about Caralee's condition. I didn't understand why. She looked healthier than she had with Miguel.

I soothed her worry, explaining about the arrival of an Earth ship. I didn't mention weapons.

Dokófray knows? I asked Koosk. But I knew that Burska would have told him. Did their high-tech include retaliatory weapons? But these were our people, probably coming to save the human children who'd been left behind when my father's ship took off for Butterfly. Surely, they wouldn't fire weapons on us. That would defeat the whole purpose of having come to save the kids.

"What do Burska and Dokófray want us to do?"

"Sleep. Be with Caralee. Stay together and remain nearby."

That I would be happy to do. I threw my arm around my family, hugging both Miguel and Caralee closer. Then we headed for bed.

In the morning, I made sure that the new children we'd brought were apportioned correctly. Twelve kids for the six newbies. So, each would be responsible for fostering two children. Of course, they were easy to take care of in stasis, and Dokófray might delay awakening them with a strange ship approaching, but at least it was a beginning. The huts the guys had been building were not finished, but there was enough of a framework to show that they were individual dwellings. The kids were taken there and set in the corners,

"How will we get enough food for everyone?" Sally asked.

Good question, for which I had no answer, but I was confident that Burska was working on it. She'd provide. Of course, while the kids were still in stasis, that was one problem we didn't have to contend with yet.

"Meeting in ten," I announced, knowing that our latest problem needed to be explained. I didn't know if I was supposed to tell the group, but I thought it would be better for them to know what was going on than to have bombs or something dropping on them without being prewarned.

The kids' expressions were not as glum, perhaps as mine. Perhaps Patsy said what they were all thinking. "Maybe they've come to get us, and that's a good thing."

It was a drop-in moment for Dokófray. "Not good thing. You stay. You needed by Buska. No leave. We fight human ship. No release anyone."

"We don't get to vote?" Leonardo said, reverting to his norm of perpetual rabble-rouser.

"No vote," Dokófray said. "They go away, or they die."

That silenced everyone. No one had expected violence from the supposedly peace-loving aliens.

"Please don't hurt them," Caralee cried out. "Send them to Butterfly or back to Earth. Please."

Dokófray gave her his full attention, then bowed. "We try, Caralee. We try."

Caralee

Nothing happened the rest of the day. It felt like a free day with no working, no traveling to get food, and everyone recuperating. Theoretically, everyone was doing whatever they felt like. Except the tension in the air had turned friends into growling opponents. Dokófray broke up a fight between Lance and Leonardo. Then later, Leonardo had a fight with Matthew. The girls were quiet. Sally kept sniveling about missing her parents. Patsy and Bonnie hung together, but their faces showed little goodwill for anyone.

By the time Lord Vagabond had taken over the sky, beaming his flare of brightness, I think everyone was thankful for bed. Only it wasn't a restful sleep that night.

Speeta's egg sac had been on the wall for a few weeks. That night, it burst and out flowed not the fifty babies we'd been told, but hundreds. Miguel startled us awake with his laughter. A few baby spiders circled about, then bedded down beside Speeta and Koosk, but most sped out the door as fast as their chubby little legs could carry them. A little while later there were screams issued from the huts across the way, so we knew in which direction at least some of the spiders had gone.

We calmed Miguel. He wanted to get down and play with the baby spiders who had decided to stay with us. Maybe he knew that one of them would be his. Storma, I think. But Caralee nursed him back into sleepiness. Then everything quieted, and we drifted back into sleep. But more screams sounded. I got up to check on it, doubting that the baby spiders were still shaking up the girls.

It was snowing.

The new huts had no roof over them, so I imagined the occupants were getting cold. I called out, urging them to come join us in our hut. In a minute, they all came rushing in, complaining about the cold and wondering why Burska had decided to punish them. Although I doubted that was the case, I turned to Koosk to ask what was going on. He was already conversing with Burska.

The girls crowded into bed with Caralee and Miguel, leaving me out in the cold with the guys, but I pulled out spare blankets, and we huddled shoulder to shoulder.

In a moment, Koosk turned to me. I forced myself out of the warmth of the huddle and went to Koosk to hear what was going on. It was bad.

The Earthers had turned on some kind of machine that inhibited Burska, causing her weather modifier to break, or at least not to operate correctly. The image I was shown did not clarify the difference.

"So what now?" I asked.

Burska gives permission to make fire. You must all keep warm. Children not endangered. Stasis protects. Insulates.

That was good to know. I had forgotten about them.

"Okay, guys, get wood. We're making a huge bonfire. We just got permission. The human ship caused this. It did something to Burska, but it will stop soon. She's repairing it."

The males were all shivering, none of them eager to leave the hut, but they got up without complaint, wrapping the extra blanket around them, and marched out. We had lots of wood around. No collection needed, but the wood was piled high with snow already. Not a good thing for starting a fire, and we had no matches.

I remembered about rubbing rocks together, but I couldn't get a spark. Each of the guys tried it. No luck. Wood piled for warmth, but no fire. Dokófray always seemed to have an ear to the ground. He popped out of nowhere, shivered, and said, "here." Whatever he did to the wood, it burst into flames. Snowdrift was no longer a problem.

We waited a moment to call the girls, but as if they sensed the heat, they came outside, massed in one grouping. In a moment, they were all sitting, arching into the heat, rubbing cold hands together and savoring the warmth. Caralee handed Miguel to me. "I have to visit the bushes," she said.

"I'll go with you," Patsy and Sally said. Then Bonnie cried out, too. "Okay, mass pee party," she said, making them all giggle.

They headed out. I hoped not going far, but I knew they wouldn't linger away from the fire. In a minute, they were headed back. Then Caralee suddenly screamed.

She slipped on the mushy ice and fell. I shoved Miguel at Leonardo, who happened to be sitting next to me and ran to my wife's side. She was sobbing.

"It hurts, Danuel."

I reached down and picked her up. I was in a query as to whether to return her to the fire or carry her back to the bed.

"The hut, Daniel. Take me back to our bed."

I understood her words perfectly, but the voice that issued them was in a panic.

"It hurts, Danuel. I think I'm going to lose Alexandro. Get help, please."

Koosk was there in a second. He sent out the broadcast for Dokófray and the herd spider, Dakowah. I'd never asked the doctor's name. I'd been too busy delivering Miguel.

Both were there before the shivers hit me. I ignored them and started heaping spiderweb blankets atop my wife, but Dakowah only removed them. "Do you need venom?" he asked me.

"No. Tell me what you need me to do. How can we save Caralee and Alexandro? I'll do anything you want."

Good, the spider said, sinking deep into my mind. *Lay down beside her. Take her into your arms. Give her your warmth.*

No hesitation. I was holding my darling wife two seconds after his order.

This was foreseen, Danuel. Remember? She will be okay, but she cannot leave the bed. Not if she wants to keep this child. She cannot get up even for her basic needs. Understand?

Of course, I replied. *Anything.*

Dakowah tore back a strip of the cobweb trousers Caralee was wearing, then, using his fangs, bit into the skin of her thigh. Caralee screamed, then sobbed, the venom spreading down and around her lower parts.

"Danuel," she cried out.

"I know. I am here. I will always be here at your side, my darling one."

"It burns."

I kissed her cheek. "I know. I remember," I said.

She whimpered once more, then slowly sank into sleep. I held her tightly, brushing hair out of her eyes, caressing her face, kissing the now peaceful lips.

"Thank you, Dakowah," I said, looking up, but the herd spider was gone. Only Dokófray remained.

"He hear you, Danuel. He know."

"How do I keep Caralee warm, Dokófray?"

"Burska in repairs. I make bonfire here, but not safe. I take up to ship?"

"No. Dakowah said not to move her. We have to stay here."

Dokófray was silent a moment, and then he disappeared.

A few minutes passed, and he'd brought some mechanical device that growled ominously. "Burska not like this," he said, but he turned it toward the bed, and I could feel the warmth emanating from it.

"But we don't have electricity," I cried out. Dokófray said nothing. He'd popped back out again.

I lay there, feeling warm and grateful for friends. Yes, Dokófray and Dakowah. Koosk and Speeta, and the newbie six. And then I remembered how Burska had let us build a bonfire, so I added Burska to my list as well.

You are welcome, First Father, Burska said, and I would have engaged her in conversation, but I was already drifting off. The night had been long, but sleep had been little.

Caralee

It was embarrassing to wake up Danuel, but I didn't know what else to do. Both Dokófray and Dakowah had made me promise not to leave the bed, but I urgently needed the bushes, and I couldn't do what I needed to do without leaving it.

"You are awake," Danuel said. "How are you feeling? Are you in pain?"

"No. Yes. I have to pee."

Danuel crawled out of bed. I thought he was going to pick me up and cart me outside, but he didn't. He returned in a second with a big turtle shell. "Sorry, baby, but it's gotta be like this for a while," he said, slipping it underneath me.

"I can't do this," I said. But Alexandro kicked at that moment, and the pee slipped out. "Ick," I said. "This is awful, Danuel. This is too . . ."

"Shhh," he said. "I love you. I'll do whatever is needed."

I felt mortified, but the shell was not comfortable, so it was also a relief to have it removed.

He left to empty the shell, and I lay there thinking about what I'd do when I had to do the other. Pee was bad enough.

"Knock knock," Patsy said, and I heard the other two girls giggling. I guess the lack of a doorbell was kind of a funny thing. Maybe I'd laugh later.

"Come in," I said, but I really didn't feel comfortable with them visiting. Miguel was nursing for one thing, and for another, I was now a total invalid.

"We're sorry about your accident," Sally said.

"You and the baby are okay, right?" Bonnie asked.

The other shushed her like they weren't sure if the answer was a positive one or not.

"Yes. We're both okay, but I'm in total bed rest. That's a big bummer. No sleepover like Bonnie promised me. No swimming. No . . ."

"It doesn't matter," Bonnie said. "That can wait."

"Hey, it's warm in here. How did that happen?"

"Dokófray," I said, as did they, all in the same moment.

"Being the herd spider princess certainly helps, doesn't it,' Bonnie said, giving me that look of hers, half joking, half serious.

"You promised you'd be nice," Sally said, scowling at her.

"It's okay," I told them. I know the herd spiders call me that. I don't know why, though. Even Speeta wouldn't tell me. "Hey, I heard you screaming last night when the baby spiders marched out."

"Oh, did you have to remind me?" Patsy said, sitting down on the foot of the bed, followed by two more plops as the others did the same thing.

"Yeah, they paraded into our sleeping area as if they owned the place. One climbed into Bonnie's hair. That was the loudest scream you heard," Sally laughed.

"You weren't laughing when one crawled up your arm," Patsy said. "I wanted to keep my spider. It was really, really cute, but after it checked me out, it took off."

I nodded. "Yeah, they have to grow up a bit. The older herd spiders will teach them stuff, and then they'll come back. I bet you anything that they were there to meet you. That way, they'll recognize you when they return. Those will be your herd spiders."

"You mean like Koosk?"

"And Speeta?"

Sally and Patsy. I could already recognize their voices without looking, and of course, Bonnie, I'd never fail to identify her voice – half sarcasm and half self-doubt and mistrust. Bonnie had been hurt. She had huge mental scars. It would take a long time before she opened to the rest of us, before she trusted us fully.

"Ladies," Danuel said from the doorway. "Did you eat your fruit already? Is it okay if I bring in Caralee's?"

They all stood up, ready to leave.

"Thanks for the visit, " I said. "I'm going to be bored out of my head in the next weeks. Could you come visit . . . often? Like every day. Like most of the day?"

Bonnie came over and kissed my cheek. I think it startled both of us. Then she moved back and said, "As toasty warm as it is in here, I'm moving in. Sorry, Danuel, you're on your own."

Everyone laughed, and Bonnie flounced out, followed by Patsy and Sally. At the door, Sally paused. "Danuel, anytime you want us to do something or help out in some way, let us know. We're here for you." She looked back at me, then winked. "You behave yourself, Caralee. No wild belly dancing."

Danuel

The first thing Caralee wanted to know was about the Earth ship. I had no information. Koosk and Dokófray had been gone all day. The weather was back to normal. I knew that much. I looked for Speeta, but she was gone, too. It was strange that I sometimes resented the spiders' constant presence, but now I missed them. I wanted information.

"Are the others still bickering?" she asked next. I nodded. "Yes, they've been keeping Dokófray busy breaking up their fights. I guess we need to get Flistercrokta back down here. We need some more: *Voice gently modulated, firm, polite.*"

"Yeah, and *Atmosphere signifies.* That's my favorite. I used to think they were telling us get on our ship and fly home."

I slipped into bed, sliding in close. "If I *modulate my voice, firm and polite,* will you kiss me?"

She giggled. "I don't think that's how it goes, Danuel," but she offered me her lips, and I took full advantage. Miguel was tucked in beside her, asleep. I was careful not to squish him as I luxuriated in the feel of having Caralee beside me.

"Í can't . . ."

"I know," I said. "We'll have to pretend that I've come to court you."

"My parents wouldn't like you crawling into bed with me, then," she said, giggling.

"Knock knock." It sounded like Matthew. "I called out for him to come in, and they all popped through the pseudo door.

"Whoops, did we come at a SUPER bad time?" Leonard asked, sneering like he was seeing something we might not want him to see.

"This is my permanent position for the next month," Caralee said. "Anytime you visit, you'll find me in bed, so get used to it, Leonardo."

"That's my girl," I said, planting another kiss on her lips for her spunkiness.

"We found some flowers," Lance said. "We thought, since this is like the new hospital ward, that it might be appropriate to bring you some."

I reached out and took them, then handed them to my wife. They were the orange flowers we sometimes saw along the trail of the woods. Not particularly sweet smelling, but they were pretty.

She gushed over their beauty, making me feel sorry that I'd never brought her any. I chided the guys about showing off one of my many faults. They laughed in a rather embarrassed way. Seeing us in bed together had really impacted them negatively. I tried again.

"You guys know anything about the human ship? Any more bomb threats?"

"They aren't going to bomb us. We're human. It's the alien planet they're attacking," Leonardo said with a hint of his former brazen argumentativeness.

"You mean the one that we're still on?" I asked. "Yeah, what the ship does to the planet is going to affect us, right?"

"Not if . . ."

Dokófray poked his nose (and the rest of his body) into the conversation at that moment. "Another fight?"

Lance thrust himself in front of Leonardo. "We were just visiting Caralee. We brought her flowers, see?"

I'm not sure if Dokófray understood the policy of bringing flowers to the sick, but he nodded. "Good. Flowers better than fists."

"We would never use a fist on Caralee," Matthew said, then realized that Dokófray was only kidding.

Silence met that response. I think it worried Dokófray that Matthew would even suggest such an idea. "Where is Koosk. And Speeta?"

I shrugged. I'd been wondering the same thing. Both of them gone at the same time. I hope that didn't meant they were trying to make another egg sac. We didn't need more baby spiders crawling around.

"What is happening with the human ship? Has it stopped doing whatever it did before?" Caralee asked.

Dokófray peered down at her. "You better?" he asked.

She nodded, then waited for her question to be answered, always a fifty-fifty proposition.

"No, get out of bed. You stay."

She nodded. "Yes, I'm bed grounded."

We all laugh, and Dokófray turned to stare at each of us. "I do not understand. Ground is to walk. Bed is to sleep. You must not sleep on ground. You must stay in bed."

I interceded. "Parents ground their kids when they do something wrong. It means the kids can't leave their room. Caralee was making a joke about how she's been grounded, Dokófray. She is not getting out of bed. She promised you."

The alien looked at me like I'd said something really strange. Perhaps I had. Child rearing didn't seem like something Dokófray knew a lot about. He writhed his pedipalps, indicating that the subject was slightly upsetting.

He turned back to Caralee. "We send human ship to Butterfly. It bother no more."

"At least not until it can return to do something else to us," Leonardo said with a sneer.

"You be with Patsy. Need more Patsy. Attitude not good."

"Yeah, that's kind of what she told me. She said I'm a troublemaker and needed to grow up. I'm working on the latter."

"Ship not return," Dokófray said. "Fuel gone. Ship land. Go nowhere."

Caralee smiled. "Thank you, Dokófray. I know you could have killed them. I am so grateful that you didn't."

"Conciliation drives from assessment. Solution goal oriented."

"I'm not sure that was goal-oriented for them," Matthew said before he caught himself and apologized to Dokófray. "Sorry, I was just thinking out loud."

"Atmosphere signifies," Dokófray stated, and Danuel and I broke into laughter.

"Sorry, Dokófray. It was just that Danuel and I were just saying that before the guys walked in. That was my favorite line."

I guess Dokófray had decided that Caralee was doing okay. He popped out a second later, not mentioning any other Buskan dictates.

Leonardo

Dokófray was pretty weird, but he got one thing right. I needed to find Patsy and make amends. As she'd said, it was going to be a dry existence if I didn't work on our relationship. And as Dokófray said, *Conciliation derives from assessment. Solution goal-oriented.*

I wasn't sure any assessment was needed. Patsy had already told me exactly what was needed. But the solution to my problem was definitely goal-oriented. I needed Patsy on my side. I needed her to be my girl. I needed Patsy.

The first thing I'd do, I thought to myself. *Atmosphere signifies.* It was time to pick some more flowers and build a better atmosphere. Wasn't that what wooing was all about?

Patsy

I hadn't spoken to Leonardo since I'd put him down so harshly while we were out picking up the children. The guy deserved it . . . and more. Just because he was the most handsome guy I'd ever seen didn't mean that I'd let him mold my life into something filled with sarcastic exchanges and nastiness. He'd have to learn what was socially okay in order to get along with people, or I seriously wasn't going along with this whole mating scenario.

I was just thinking those thoughts when along came Romeo with a humble expression on his face and a handful of orange flowers. I already knew about those. We called them Skunk Flora for obvious reasons. But the boy was trying. I had to give him that. So when he handed them to me, I took them, pretended to sniff at them like a girl was supposed to do, and thanked him for his gift.

Behind me, I could hear the girls snickering, but I ignored them and walked over to the side, away from them. Of course, Leonardo followed.

Again, I thanked him for the flowers, but I didn't take another whiff. The first one, even though I was trying not to inhale, would make my nose ineffective for the rest of the day.

"Where have you been all day?" I asked, then could have bitten my tongue. I should have pretended I didn't know he was gone. I should have . . . oh, heck. Not going to do the pretending. Besides, I wanted to know what he'd been up to.

His eyes didn't reflect any chagrin at my questioning him. He seemed glad to know that I cared enough to ask.

"The guys and I went to talk with Caralee. We brought her some of those flowers. We hoped that would cheer her up. She's in total bed rest for a month. That won't be easy for her."

I nodded. I couldn't help sniffing the flowers again. How could something so pretty smell so bad? One of life's mysteries, obviously.

"Yeah, I know. We visited her, too. Was Danuel there with her?"

Leonardo nodded, then spurted out as if appalled. "He was in bed with her. We almost left when we saw that. Pretty embarrassing, but he'd told us to come in."

"You can be assured he wasn't doing what you're thinking. They don't want to lose the baby, and any kind of movement is a no-no."

I swear the man blushed — only a little, though. Maybe I imagined it, but no, there was still heightened color in his cheeks. So, he wasn't the player he insinuated he'd been. Really, that hadn't made much sense anyway. How could someone be outrageously chasing girls when to do so would end you up in the bad cell? With the Mate List, you only got to go out with your intended, not play the field.

Leonardo had just earned points in my *will I, won't I* approach to this whole pairing concept. He was still pretty iffy, but the arrow was wavering. He was awful cute, and those eyes of his were dreamy.

Nerves of steel, I told myself. This is a lifetime commitment, and I was going to make him climb a very steep hill to get to the top.

"Do you want to take a walk to the river?" he asked. "There's a great lookout point there, and we just might see the river dragon Bonnie was talking about."

He had me at walk to the river, but I just nodded and acted nonchalant.

Danuel

Since the troublesome ship was gone, we decided to go ahead and wake up the kids. Dokófray showed up just as Leonardo was asking how we were going to do that without a technical wizard-alien.

He'd been holding Patsy's hand, but with his wisecrack, she released it and turned away. I didn't think his words were that bad, but it pushed some button that Patsy had installed, so I guess he paid the price for not modulating his words a bit.

We were heading to the new huts, the half-finished huts, where the kids had been placed. Lance had suggested we hold up in waking the kids until we'd finished the huts, but the girls were eager to start being little mothers, so today was the day. I felt bad for Caralee. She desperately wanted to be there for the awakening, but that was out of the question. I promised to give her all the details when we got back.

Koosk and Speeta were both with her in case she needed something. I promised her I'd be back in a minute.

We started first on Sally and Lance's new kids. Sally had been given a boy named Joey and a girl named Francine. Lance helped with Joey, making sure the boy didn't tumble over as Dokófray undid his stasis. The boy was ten, the girl twelve, at least that's what Dokófray told us, but the girl looked younger than twelve, maybe closer to the boy's age.

Waking them up was a repetition of what Caralee and I had gone through with her parents. The kids felt sick and dizzy at first, then unsure about what was going on. "In a fog," Sally said, remembering how it had been for her. The two kids took to Sally right off, the girl hugging her like she'd found her mommy. Joey was a little standoffish, but you could tell he was appraising Lance and liking what he saw.

It would be nice to have given them more time, but we moved on to Patsy's two children. Tommy was seven, the youngest of all the children. Apparently, his parents were dead, and he had been living with an elderly aunt who didn't survive the stasis. She was the only one killed by the process. Dokófray was very upset and seemed crushed by the failure.

Anyway, that's why Tommy had remained on Burska instead of heading off to Butterfly with the others his age. His new brother was Billy, who was a younger child, too, at only eight. His parents, Dokófray said, had been abusive. It sounded like Patsy and Leonardo would have their hands full.

Last for the day were Bonnie's two; Samuel and Christine were both twelve. The procedure was repeated with them. Samuel seemed more hazy than some of the others. He could hardly stand. Christine seemed to take it all in stride. Her big eyes looked about, then she said,

"Where are my parents?" When we explained, she didn't cry or say anything other than, "Oh." It was rather strange, I thought, but all people differed in how they acted.

That was the last of them for the day. The guys' remaining children had been placed in the farthest hut. They would be awakened a week later if everything went well with these.

"Are we calling these their children or their younger siblings?" I asked Dokófray.

Unhelpfully, he merely shrugged. Something I'd have to discuss with the six, something we should have batted around earlier. Maybe it didn't matter. Maybe the kids would just call them by their first names. That was a thought. I decided that was my choice if I had a vote in the situation.

"We'll meet at campfire for dinner," I said, and everyone nodded their heads, but that didn't take their minds off acquainting themselves with the little ones.

I scurried back to Caralee, but I was thinking about the changes we'd be encountering. We'd be needing more food, bigger houses, clothing, blankets . . .

Bonnie

If I'd had any qualms about Matthew, they dissolved when I saw him with Samuel and Christine. Both kids were still in the dazed stage. Matthew kept his voice low and talked with them about how their parents hadn't been able to take in the nutrition of the planet and had needed to leave for another planet, one called Butterfly.

"But why did they leave us here?" Samuel asked.

"They didn't want to," Matthew said, "but Burska, that's the name of the planet, not Beatnik, wanted to offer you this great opportunity of living in a place with lots of freedom and where you get to ride herd spiders. In fact, if you're nice to the spiders, you'll get your own herd spider to ride all around."

"But my parents are gone," Christine said. "They were going to make me marry someone the List chose. They said I had to do it or else."

"But not for a long time. You're only twelve, right?"

Christine's eyes were roaming all around, not really believing the change she'd undergone. "My parents said that the moment I turned fifteen. They wanted to get rid of me because I ate too much."

"You're not fat," Samuel said. "Why would they say that?"

Christine started to cry. I hugged her to me, and she didn't pull away. "Here, we eat fruit from the trees. You only need one, and you get super full, and it tastes really good."

She nodded. "I'll try not to eat too much," she said. "I don't want you to kick me out."

I felt like crying. This was so sad. "Here, nobody gets kicked out. You'll always have a home with Matthew and me."

"Are you a couple? Are you married already?"

Oh, dear. Was that going to be a problem? I looked at Matthew and didn't know what to say.

"We will be," Matthew said. "We're still courting right now. But when we get married, then you and Samuel can be our children, if that's okay with you. Or you can call us Matthew and Bonnie if you prefer. I'll let you think about it, okay?"

We talked a bit more, finding out that Samuel didn't like herd spiders because they scared him, but we assured him these were friendly spiders. He still looked uncertain.

"Are there other children left behind?" Christine asked.

"There's a girl your age. Her name is Francine. And there are three boys who are seven, eight, and ten. But more will be coming next week."

"Will there be school?" Samuel asked.

"Probably, but not for a while. We don't have books, pencils, or paper, so it will have to be a very different kind of school." Matthew told him.

"You're very pretty," Christine said. "I bet your parents loved you."

"I think you're pretty, too," I said, although right now she looked just sad and weepy. But that would change. Things would get a lot better for Christine. I planned to make sure of that.

Leonardo

Tommy, the younger boy, was pretty upset to learn that his aunt had died.

"My mommy and da died, too," he said.

"You're lucky. I wish mine had. They were mean."

Okay, that was a socker punch. I couldn't imagine what Billy had gone through.

"None of that here. We're going to take care of you now," Patsy said, and her smile was so sweet they both kind of fell into it. I understood the feeling.

"My name's Leonardo, I said, "and the pretty one there is Patsy."

Patsy looked down in embarrassment. Hadn't anyone told her that before? She was a blonde-haired, blue-eyed doll, but of course, I didn't say that. I'd gotten smacked for saying less.

"You are pretty," Tommy said. "Will you marry me when I grow up?"

Billy laughed. "She can't marry you. She's married to him. They're going to be our parents, silly. You can't marry your mom."

"Okay," Tommy said. "That's okay, then. If you're my mom, you won't go away, right? You'll stay with us forever and ever?"

"Actually." I could tell that Patsy was about to tell them we weren't married. I stopped her with my finger on her mouth.

"The truth, boys? We're not married yet. We were waiting for you to wake up so you could be at our family wedding. Is that okay?"

Patsy shook her head at me. I could see there was still doubt in her eyes, but if we already had a family, we couldn't **not** get married, could we? And the boys were already whooping and hollering over being at our family wedding. Obviously, they agreed with me that it was a super idea.

Now, if only I could convince Patsy of that.

Chapter Nine

Sally

I've got to admit this was the scariest moment of my life. Not waking up to find that aliens had invaded and our parents were gone. Not finding out that I had a new List Mate, but this moment, building a relationship with two kids. Lance was looking calm as he explained to Joey and Francine about their parents having been taken to another planet and us being their new parents.

The boy looked doubtful, probably figuring that we'd kidnapped them and were crazy or something. Ten year old Joey put up his dukes and was about to slug Lance, telling him he better take us back to his parents or else. Francine wasn't saying anything. She just looked hesitant.

"I remember the aliens," she said to Joey. "They looked like herd spiders, except they came down in spaceships."

"I remembered that, too. Only Dad said it was all a trick. He said there wasn't such a thing as aliens and that we should just ignore them. I guess that didn't work, right?" Joey said.

"I saw them shoot my parents," Francine said. Then, I think one sneaked up behind me and shot me. It hurt. I remember that, but nothing else."

Lance was nodding. "That's what happened to me, too. The aliens put me into stasis like you. Then they brought us here, and now we're supposed to help you adjust. We're supposed to be like your parents, you know?"

"I'm called Sally, and he's Lance. The guys have been working on building houses, but this one's not finished yet. But that's where we're sleeping. It doesn't get cold here, so that works out okay. It snowed a few days ago, and we had to build a bonfire, but that was kind of fun. Except for one of the girls, Caralee, she fell on the ice. She has to stay in bed for a while. Maybe we can visit her tomorrow. She's really nice."

Francine nodded. "Yeah, I fell on the ice once, too. It hurt my bottom."

"I've fallen lots. It's no big deal. Why does she have to stay in bed?" Joey asked.

I looked up at Lance, ready for him to take over, but he just nodded, urging me on.

"She's pregnant, having a baby, so it wasn't good for the baby for her to fall."

"My mom got pregnant, " Francine said, "but she lost the baby. That happens sometimes. She cried a lot after that and never got better. She went to bed and didn't want to get up. Dad finally made her get up, but she just dodged him and went back to bed. I hope your friend doesn't do that."

"Caralee isn't losing the baby. She's going to be fine," Sally said. "But the doctor told her she has to stay in bed. After she has the baby, she'll be up again, though."

Maybe I wouldn't bring Francine to see Caralee. There was something about the girl that told me she was on the edge of depression. I guess her mom staying in bed all the time had been pretty damaging.

"What do you like to do, Joey," I asked, mainly to get off the subject of dead babies.

Joey, once wound up, didn't seem to have an off button. He told us more about baseball than I'd ever wanted to hear. Lance was okay with that. The two of them seemed right in tune. While they were talking about quality balls and bats, Francine and I skipped from conversation to conversation, looking for something we could share.

Francine did not like to swim, sing, play games, watch movies, read books, or get together with friends. It appeared like she had zero interests. How was that possible?

"What did you and your daddy do?"

"Mostly, we cooked dinner and cleaned the house together. I had to do all the laundry. He showed me how once, then it was my chore."

Okay. That sounded like a not-very fun or exciting existence.

"What was your favorite school subject?"

"I never went to school. Dad said he'd teach me everything I needed to know, but he was always too busy or too tired. Mom used to teach me how to read, but after she lost the baby, she wouldn't even do that."

I thought school was mandatory on Beatnik, but I guess there weren't any folks enforcing it. Government was pretty low-key, or rather it used to be when we had a government — before Beatnik became Burska.

I listened in for a moment to Lance and Joey. Still going strong in baseball.

"Did you have any other siblings, Francine?"

"What are those?"

Don't look exasperated, I told myself. Uneducated, unhappy, bad life. Poor kid. I had my work cut out for me.

"Brothers and sisters?"

She shook her head.

"Cousins?"

Another head shake

"So there was no one to play with?"

"Dad said there was too much to do to be wasting time, and no one lived close anyway."

"Francine, things are going to be very different here. For one thing, I'm going to make sure you learn to have fun. And forget doing chores all day. We're going to find you some friends and let you experience having a good time."

I wished that had brought a smile to her face, but her lips were pursed like she was about to argue, and her only facial expression seemed to be a permanent scowl.

Caralee

They were having a party out at the campfire, this time again with no campfire, and I wasn't part of it. I'd never gotten to do much of that growing up, but now that I had friends in the group, I wanted to savor things like parties and being all cuddly with my husband. I lay in bed feeling sorrier and sorrier for myself until Koosk came over. He lowered his big body down to my level, then pressed his head against me.

Short time only. Soon, friends come in. You laugh, you tell stories. You have fun.

It was cool that Koosk was talking to me, but I didn't know if he was right. Maybe this would be my future from now on. Lying in bed with babies growing in my stomach.

No. I call Danuel.

"Don't, Koosk. Danuel needs to be there, checking on things, seeing how the kids are doing, looking for problems."

I must leave.

The moment he left, Speeta sat up and sauntered over. *We visited the children last night. Not initiate more hatchlings. These three spiders keep me from sleeping. They tickle me without stop.*

Well, it was a relief that there would be no more egg sacs for a while, but I thought it might be rude to say that.

Koosk dragged in Danuel. I got kisses.

"I told you not to call him, Koosk," I scolded the huge herd spider.

He needed here.

It is good to be needed, Daniel sent.

Daniel had to do the bedpan turtle shell again, then left to empty it. When he came back, he brought someone with him.

"Hi, Sally, who is this?"

"Francine, meet Caralee."

I thought at that moment how I really needed chairs in our hut, but like always, Sally sat down at the end of the bed. Francine, who I remembered was twelve, sat down beside her. Francine had two long braids. They looked like she'd slept in them. I wondered if she knew how to braid them herself. Had her mother always done so for her?

"I was telling Francine about how you're having a baby. She wanted to meet you."

"Hi, Francine. I'm so glad you've come to live with us. We needed some brightness around here."

But in that moment, the feelings I was getting from Francine crystallized. Any brightness I got was not going to come from this girl, not for a long time. She was sadness incarnate.

"I get very lonely in bed," I told the child. "I am glad you came to see me. In fact, earlier, I was feeling downtrodden because you were all outside partying, and I was inside by myself. Do you ever feel like that, Francine?"

"What is downtrotting?"

"It's when you feel sad. I was sad because I was in here alone."

"Yes," Francine said.

I looked over at Sally, wondering what to say next. She picked up on the cue. "We're going to teach Francine how to have fun. She worked all the time and never had time for play."

I nodded. Okay. "Do you like to play checkers?"

Francine shook her head. His messy braids flew from side to side. Her nose crinkled as if the idea of checkers was appalling.

"Have you ever played checkers?" Sally asked.

Again, Francine shook her head. She smiled then, but only for a second. "You're like a young child. Did you hit your head?" she asked me.

I burst out laughing at that. "Oh, Danuel would have loved to hear you say that."

"What, darling?" he said. "What would I want to hear?"

Francine stood up and made a curtsey. "I'm sorry, sir. I didn't ask. Is it okay to sit here?"

Danuel froze. I won't say his mouth dropped because Danuel didn't do things like that, but his shock at her calling him *sir* flew across the room and hit me in the face.

"Please," he said. "if you wanted to swing from the rafters to entertain my wife, I'd be happy. She needs someone to make her laugh."

"I'm sorry, sir. I don't know what rafters are."

"First off, my name is Danuel. Dan is okay, too."

"Yes, sir."

"No, not sir, Danuel."

Francine curtseyed again. She obviously didn't understand that he was trying to take away her fear.

"I've asked Francine to play checkers with me. Do we still have all the pieces? It's been so long since Lissie left."

"Who was Lissie?" Francine asked.

"My little sister. She was only four, so she had to leave with our parents. I miss her a lot. She used to love to play checkers. Tic tac toe, too. Oh, and other games. I haven't thought of that in months."

"I'll get the checker set together, and I think you could play tic tac toe in a turtle bowl of sand. Maybe other games, too."

"You are the sweetest, kindest husband in all the world. But where's our son?"

Danuel laughed. "Leonardo is holding him. He did so when you got hurt, and it seems that Patsy was impressed; now, he keeps asking if he can hold Miguel. He's wooing Patsy, you know."

I laughed so hard at that Alexandro tried to join in. His foot kicking my insides went halfway through my skin — or at least, it felt like that.

Danuel sat down on the side of the bed. "Sally, you're being extra quiet tonight."

"To be honest, every time I see you two interacting, I just want to sit back and enjoy it. My parents were cold as . . . well, the falling snow that hit us recently. My parents hardly ever spoke to each other and certainly never touched. It's like role modeling I'm absorbing so one day . . ."

I giggled. "Hear that, Danuel? We're role models."

"I like it, too," Francine said, surprising everyone because she'd actually volunteered something. A positive something.

"Do you think I could ever get some paper and a pencil? I used to have a sketchpad, and I liked to draw in it."

"You're like Lissie," she exclaimed. "My sister used to pick up a stick everywhere we went, then she drew in the dirt and in the sand. She made sand castles, too, with moats and animals in the moats. But her favorite thing to do was to draw. I bet some of her drawings are still down there. I could take you to see them."

The sudden silence made her gasp. "Whoops, I forgot. Bedrest. Well, Sally could take you down there to see them. It doesn't have to be me."

Francine's eyes lit up. "Really? I could draw in sand. I never knew that. Or dirt?"

How had she not realized that? What kind of monster took all the pleasure out of being a child?

"I think it's time to see what Lance and Joey are doing. Joey is into baseball," Sally said, standing up.

Danuel laughed. "No kidding. He's already got Tommy, Billy, and Samuel signing up for his baseball team. He wants us to hurry up and wake up more kids so he can have two teams."

"Bye, Francine," Caralee said, "Please come back and play games with me. You could do some drawings, too, and show them to me. I'd love to see. I have absolutely no artistic ability. Could you teach me to draw?"

"Wow, slow down, my darling. Give the girl time to breathe."

He was still chuckling when they left, but I wanted to tell him about Francine, the saddest girl I'd ever known.

I was still talking about her when Leonardo came in with Miguel. The baby had decided he wanted milk. I knew he couldn't be hungry, but I never turned him down.

"Do you think you could get Francine and Christine together?" I asked. "Francine really needs cheering up."

Leonardo smiled. "That's a great idea. Maybe they can cheer each other up. Christine's parents couldn't wait to push her off into marriage. She said they wanted to get rid of her because she ate too much. She's on a downer slide, too."

He glanced back at Danuel. "Boss, if it's okay, we're taking the day off from work tomorrow. Joey says we have to have a game right away, and my Samuel agrees 100%."

"Super idea," I said, laughing, although I don't think Danuel liked being called boss.

"That sounds doable. We'll call it Kids' Day," Danuel said.

"Sounds more like boy's day to me," I said, slightly irritated. Why were there only two girls in the first group? Why so many boys?"

Both guys shrugged. I knew they hadn't been the ones to pick the children, so I couldn't blame them. I wondered how many girls we'd find still in stasis.

Danuel

The girls gathered in our hut. The guys all went to play baseball. The biggest problem is that we had no ball, and what we pieced together came apart. Joey thought we should put a rock in the center, but I vetoed that. The bat stick worked just fine, although I worried about splinters flying into someone's eyes.

We tried using a kind of pinecone I'd found in the woods, but it shattered at the first hit, collapsing into tiny fragments. Likewise, filling spiderweb material with sand made another disaster, although a rather amusing one if you looked at the kids' faces after the first explosion. Finally, depleted of ideas, I offered my shoe.

The poor thing was falling apart, having survived all kinds of abuse, including frequent dunkings in mud, but it still had some rubber in it. My shoe made the first successful baseball we'd found. And the lucky part was that I had two of them. The unlucky part is that I'd be like Caralee, shoeless from then on.

The boys, including Tommy and Billy, who both had never had a single opportunity to play, had a great time. Samuel, the oldest, proved to be extremely kind to the little guys, showing them how to hold the stick for proper batting. He never once got mad when they couldn't hit anything, even a shoe the size of my huge foot. We kept throwing our pitches low to the ground, and the very nature of throwing a shoe kept our pitches slower than a turtle climbing up to its nest.

The day was a complete success, and we finished it off with a swim to both clean off the sweat and cool us down. Unfortunately, we discovered that none of the boys could swim. Not one of them. So, the lessons turned to floating in the small tide pool area where the depth of the water was only chest-high for Tommy and Billy. Billy didn't want to get in the water at first. He said it drowned people, but with Lance and Leonardo holding him up and making sure he didn't get dunked, he adapted to the idea.

Joey was something else. He had to be watched constantly. He had no fear and jumped in every time we turned our back, even though he sank and fought the water like it was attacking him.

We dined on Gorla fruit, and then I introduced the boys to Kiginoa. They thought the root was great once they got over its odd shape and ugly brownish outer surface. They asked for more but only got one small piece. I explained that even a second piece of Kiginoa would give them stomach aches.

Although one Gorla fruit was sufficient for their nutritional needs, the boys were used to eating bigger quantities, That might be a problem. I'd have to ask Dokófray about it. What else could we use to satisfy their need for big platters of food? I figured the alien would just say they needed to adapt. I remembered how Caralee and I had been hungry for a couple of days.

After the meal, the boys all bedded down right at the campfire. No reason to take them back to the unfinished huts. Besides, they thought that was special.

"Is this like camping out?" Billy asked. Then he ducked because he expected to be hit for asking *another dumb question*. Instead, Leonardo ruffled his hair and gave him a big smile. "Yep," he said. "All we need is a good ghost story."

Bad thing to say. These were kids going through some tough times, losing their parents and learning that aliens had turned them into standing statures for a year. But Leonardo had started it, so I hoped they could find a modified version of a ghost story that didn't provoke nightmares.

"Once there was a haunted house . . ."

"What's that?" Joey asked.

It was obvious from the blank expressions that these kids didn't know anything about haunted houses, and when the definition included ghosts, there was that same empty-eyed blankness.

I took over. "In a hut down by the river, four boys were curled up, ready to sleep. One of them started snoring so loudly that the others threw my shoe at him. Of course, that wasn't nice, so they all curled up again after saying they were sorry. Then when the snorer started his loud snorts and hisses, sounding like this: shhhh, snnn, shhhh, snnn, no one even heard him because they'd all fallen asleep."

Leonardo made a face. "You call that a ghost story?"

"No, I call that a putting exhausted boys to sleep story."

The other guys snickered. I got up, nodded, and headed for the hut to see what was going on with the girls.

I started to call out the knock knock we'd been voicing to gain entrance, but instead, I did a doorbell noise: Ding dong ding dong. To my knowledge, no one had a doorbell on Burska, but the video movies used them. The girls recognized the sound and had big smiles on their faces when I entered.

"Baseball game finished?" Caralee asked.

"All done, although I had to sacrifice my shoes," I said, gaining their sympathy.

"Good," Caralee said. "Now you're like me, shoeless except for the bark shoes that refuse to work well. They slippy slide all over the place."

For a moment, I worried that bad shoes had been at the root of Caralee's fall, but then I remembered she'd been barefoot. Still, making shoes was something else we'd need to work on. We needed comfortable bark shoes that didn't fall off. No doubt, the way kids grew, we'd have to become expert shoe assemblers soon. Although I remembered vids where kids never wore shoes. Maybe it wasn't that big a necessity, at least not right away.

The girls left after that. I took care of Caralee's needs and picked up Miguel from the ground where he'd been crawling about and probably pulling himself up to walk, which he loved to do. With my son in my arms, I snuggled into bed with my beautiful wife. Miguel was probably warn out from entertaining everyone. He lay quietly, his head on my chest, sucking one finger. My hand went to Caralee's big belly.

Alexandro was doing his usual kicking. I'd seen a vid on soccer once. I wondered if, instead of baseball, my newest son would be a soccer player. Or maybe he was doing karate?

I started to ask Caralee which one she thought, but she was already nodding off, exhausted by her morning's social interactions. I lay there for a moment, watching her. One of the ladies had brushed her hair until it was shiny, and she had rosy cheeks from laughing. Her lips were slightly parted as if she were just about to say something. I missed the freckles that bloomed across her nose when she got too much sun. She looked pale now. But that would change soon. I wondered how much longer before Alexandro was due. From the looks of her stomach, it must be soon. She was swollen like an over-ripe Gorla fruit, ready to burst.

I listened to Caralee's breaths as she breathed in and out. It was a rhythm I knew well, a part of me as much as the sound of her laughter and her verbal chafing at restrictions. I smiled. I still thought she was the most beautiful girl I'd ever seen. In fact, although I'd once admired the challenge in the eyes of the twelve-year-old vixen who'd teased me so brutally, the big-eyed fifteen years so full of fear, and the beautiful young bride that Dokófray had married me to, I appreciated her now more than ever. Because now she was my partner, my equal in this crazy life we were living. She was my anchor.

Migel lifted up his head to eye me. I knew that look. He wanted to give me a message. I touched his cheek with my hand to improve his receptivity, although he was still sprawled across my chest, so I didn't really need to. But my hand touch sent images flowing out immediately.

Dokófray coming. Dakowah on his way. Caralee bathed in sweat, panting. Tonight. Alexandro was coming.

When I opened my eyes, Miguel was beaming down at me. Apparently, he liked the idea of having a brand new little brother.

When Caralee woke, I brought her two Gorla fruits, urging her to eat both of them. We both knew that would cause the emptying of her bowels.

"I don't want to . . ."

But then she read my thoughts and saw that the baby was coming.

"Oh," she said. "But I hate making you deal with that."

I smiled. "Last time, my darling. Let's get this show on the road."

Another expression from my father. Caralee squinted her eyes. Her head shook once or twice, then she said, "What on Earth, on Burska, does that mean?"

I shrugged. "One of my dad's. I saw a commercial where kids were watching cartoons inside a vehicle while it was traveling down a paved road. I think that's getting a show on the road?"

"Okay, and is the baby the video or the road?"

It didn't matter. The sudden streak of fear in her eyes at being told she was going to deliver the baby had faded away. She was giggling again. My sweet Caralee.

"Miguel says that Dokófray and Dakowah are coming soon."

"On the road?" She giggled like a toddler. "I get it. Am I the show, or is it Alexandro?"

There was a ding-dong at the door, letting us know that one of the girls was asking for entrance. We both called out, "Come in."

It was Bonnie. She took one look at us and said, "The baby's coming, isn't he?"

"How did you know?" Caralee asked.

"Christine said I should check on you. She said you needed me. She had a dream that you were surrounded by herd spiders, all humming and crooning."

Bonnie surveyed our faces. "Weird dream, right? But she was right, well, except for the herd spiders. No herd spiders here. Not even the giant one who always guards you."

Our gaze instinctively darted to Lissie's old bed, where both Speeta and Koosk hung out. Bonnie was right. They'd left.

"They're probably out eating insects. No Gorla fruit for them. They prefer fat, tasty, crunchy, chitinous exoskeletons," I told them.

Both girls gave a delicious ewwww, which was the delight of every juvenile boy. I obviously didn't fit into the category of a taunting ten-year-old boy, but it must have been a throwback to my earlier years because I still found it amusing.

Dokófray showed up as Lord Tramp was rising in the sky. It was an ominously cloudy night, but the alien assured me that no rain was coming. He patted me on the back, then directed me to return to the hut. I'd just emptied and washed out the turtle shell pot and was heading back anyway.

Bonnie was still there with Caralee. They were talking about the river dragon, a subject I had mixed feelings about. Although it seemed strange that Bonnie and Lissie would have the same hallucination, the idea that a dragon lived in the river was just too far-fetched to believe. What did it eat? Were there fish in the river or crustaceans like the ones advertised on Earth? If not, then how could a huge creature fill up on the only roots of reeds and a few mosses?

Bonnie's eyes got bigger when she saw Dokófray. He represented everything negative to her in spite of the fact that he hadn't scolded her in months. Perhaps she identified him with her parents, who may not have been the most patient and loving, but then Bonnie, when she first arrived, had been an undisciplined, sarcastic rebel, much like Leonardo. If that's what her parents had seen, then I understood their harshness.

The moment Dokófray entered, Bonnie made a speedy retreat. "See you tomorrow," Bonnie said. "You can introduce me to

Alexandro." She stopped. "Do you want me to take Miguel? I could watch him for you... .?"

I thanked her for the offer but sent her on her way. Miguel would want to greet his new brother. He'd already informed me that he would remain in the hut with us during the delivery. I guess that would be hard for most people to understand, but Miguel was unique. No way to explain to why Caralee and I took his demands seriously. He was only a part-time baby. The rest of the time he was an ancient seer, informing us and guiding us along the path of Burska.

To say it was an easy birth might get me slapped, but Dakowah made sure it was a painless one. Koosk was present but didn't bite me this time. I kept out of the way of both Dokófray and Dakowah, so I guess there was no need. As before, once they'd gotten my wife on the road to the birthing process, they both disappeared. Then it was only me and about twenty herd spiders, all coming to hum Alexandro into existence outside of the womb.

Caralee thought it was funny, which made Miguel laugh as well. Then the proboscis dropped from the whole group of spiders, and all of them were making quite raucous blasts of what sounded nothing like music to me. Several of the newbies knocked at the door, perhaps concerned with the number of herd spiders or else with the noise they were making, but I sent the teens on their way, telling them that Caralee was fine but in labor.

"I'm so fine, feeling oh, so good," Caralee sang with a very unusual rock music kind of voice, not the one I often heard her using to sing lullabies to Miguel. But then, Caralee sounded ridiculously drunk. Like in the movie vids where the character drinks a whole bottle of something, then can't walk a straight line and begins to slur all their words. Not that Caralee needed to walk any lines. But she certainly seemed to enjoy her present state.

"Gonna go down to the river and float my boat, rocking the waves like a surfin' fool."

Proboscises fluttering, wiggling back and forth. Could a herd spider dance with his tongue?

More knocks at the door. Then, a doorbell ring. Bonnie, I knew.

"All right, all right," I said. "Check her out, then leave. She's busy doing the getting ready thing. She's halfway to the push."

Bonnie slipped in through the doorway, her eyes scanning the tongue-wagging spiders. She paused to take note of Koosk, who was on guard at the door, looking ferocious as a caged predator, and then, finally, turned to survey Caralee.

"Ah, sweety," Bonnie said. "What can I do to help?"

Caralee looked at her and giggled. "Gonna float my boat down the rapids of the river, holding on to the sides of the boat. Whoopie, I say. Ride them waves. Whoopie. Ride them waves. . ."

"What did you give her?" Bonnie demanded as she scooped up Miguel, who'd been sitting on the ground next to the bed.

"Spider venom. It takes away all the pain, as you can see. Leaves her feeling like laughing and giggling."

"So I see. That sounds weird to me, but I guess you did this before?"

"Kind of, but before, I was knocked out. Koosk bit me. Remember, I told you guys."

"Yeah, I remember. Okay, I'll go tell the others that everything's going well, and I'll take this little guy if you want. He doesn't need to see the blood."

"No," I said as Koosk let out a stark growl. Speeta, who almost never growled, echoed it. Speeta strode right toward Bonnie, lowering her fangs as a visible threat.

Bonnie screamed and jumped back. "They won't let me take the baby outside?" Bonnie gulped with fear-wide eyes.

"Miguel, are you able to touch her?"

The baby turned his face away from his mother to stare into Bonnie's eyes. Her already alarmed eyes widened further. "Ow," she said, but she didn't move, didn't drop her gaze away from Miguel's.

I have no idea what image he tossed at her, but I could tell that he did something that impacted her. She handed the baby to me, then headed towards the door, only stopping to turn and say. "I'm going down to play with the river dragon. He's not nearly as bizarre as you guys."

I found that puzzling. I wondered if there was any correlation to Caralee singing about floating on the river and Bonnie's departure to visit the dragon. I would have paused longer to think about it, but things were happening, and Miguel warned me it was time to get back to being a baby coach.

Three pushes later, and we had a new son. I went through the same procedures as before, except Koosk demanded the afterbirth, which seemed strange, but he took it off somewhere, leaving me to stay with Caralee, a genuinely good deal.

Baby Alexandro was as perfectly formed as Miguel, with all the necessary body parts, and knowing Caralee, I counted toes and fingers, finding them all present.

"It was strange to see blonde hair on Alexandro. I commented about that, although we'd known to expect it. "Wait until Carolina. She'll have auburn-red," Caralee said, remembering the image Miguel had shown.

Miguel, who I'd just placed on the bed, crawled immediately toward his new brother. He stood up, leaning on Caralee for balance, and said, "Xandro."

"Wow. Really good, Miguel," I said, awed by this genius child of ours.

"Judge," he added.

Okay, that made the goosebumps scurry up and down my back, but again, I smiled and said, "Good job, Miguel."

Caralee was too busy putting Alexandro to her breast. If she heard Miguel, she didn't react.

"Storma, Nartha next," Miguel said.

That I couldn't relate to, but apparently Speeta did. She strode forward touched her pads to Miguel. I caught the word soon, but that was it, so whatever meaning Miguel had, apparently, that was a herd spider thing.

"Dokófray come," Miguel suddenly said.

Was this typical? But when was anything ever typical for Miguel? I washed that thought out of my mind and waited for the knock knock. Except I forgot. No knock-knock with Dokófray. He popped into the room without a bit of fanfare.

"We have judge?"

I felt the irritation jetting all the way around the room with that remark. I once saw a cartoon with an angry cat's fur sticking up at all angles. The claws were spears of sharp. The teeth pointed arrows of rage. That was Caralee.

"The baby is named Alexandro. He is not just a judge for your ambitions. He is our son!"

Dokófray took no affront. Perhaps he realized that Caralee was not about to launch herself at him in her current state of fatigue, especially not with the baby nursing. He only bobbed his head. "Yes. Spiders not gather for any baby. They here for Miguel and Alexandro. Special birth. Like others: the doctor, the peacemaker, the caretaker."

"I'm done," Caralee said, "No more babies."

"Yes. Burska say, tired. She wait now. Doctor long time away. You say year."

"Thank you," said Caralee, but I think she was just too tired to argue further.

"Miguel not drink milk now. He eats fruit and Kiginoa."

"Why?" Caralee said. "I have enough for both of them."

"Burska say no. Miguel know. He not ask more. He eat fruit and root."

"Danuel," Caralee said, fighting off eyes that were demanding closure.

I picked up Miguel, kissed Alexandro and Caralee, then stepped away. "She needs to rest now," I told Dokófray, but when I turned to look at him, I saw that he was already gone.

"Will you guard them?" I asked Speeta.

"Of course," she issued directly into my mind.

I wanted at that moment to do nothing more than to crawl into bed with Caralee and the baby, but I needed to feed Miguel and greet the others. I had responsibilities for this new community we were making. I shot one more glance back at my wife, saw her sleep-breathing, and stepped outside.

Chapter Ten

Matthew

"Congratulations," I said, stepping forward to be the first to greet Danuel. The others crowded around, gushing similar good wishes.

"Can we see her?" Sally and Patsy wanted to know, their faces alight with fresh enthusiasm. Somehow, they made me feel ancient, a tired old man instead of someone just past twenty.

I drew in air and sought for the energy to deal with their greetings and questions. "Later, please. She's asleep right now, as is Alexandro. But everything's good."

"Back away, everyone," I said. "Can't you see he's about to drop? He's exhausted."

Sally stretched out her arms for Miguel. "Can I take him? I'll feed him some Gorla fruit."

"In a paste," I said, releasing him to her.

"No, big fruit," Miguel said, stunning everyone into silence.

"Yeah, he started talking," I said. "New thing."

Manuel took my arm and led me over to the log. "Sit down," he said. "Lance, grab a fruit, would you?"

I wasn't hungry. I just needed sleep, but I took the Gorla and bit into it. My body took over, devouring the fruit without manners, gobbling down every last bite. Juice streaked my clothes, adding to the blood splatter. I was a mess, but I no longer cared. I was just too tired to care. I sagged, leaning over to the right.

"Okay, we'll bed you down right here," I told him, helping him down into the dirt.

"Maybe we should leave this poor guy to get some rest. I bet he was up all night. Let's see what mischief Leonardo is up to," I said, laughing, but I was truthfully unsure about what Bonnie was doing while in Leonardo's proximity. The two of them had volunteered to take the kids down to the beach for some quality playtime in the sand.

I suppose I had no reason not to trust Bonnie. She and I had been sleeping in the same hut with Patsy, Leonardo, and the four kids. She'd acted like my mate for the last few days, but old doubts were apparently prone to rise up and bite us. I felt the urge to check.

I think Patsy read the worry in my eyes. She drew close and leaned over to whisper. In my ear. "Better to know before we commit, right?"

I nodded, more to be agreeable than because I accepted her philosophy.

The kids had been digging holes, not making sand castles. That was the first thing we noticed; then, we saw that the deepest hole was a finished project. They were burying Leonardo. At least the three older boys were. Tommy and Billy were sitting with Bonnie, making a moat deeper, using sticks to drag the unwanted sand into the sand pile at the end of the moat. Christine and Francine were sitting together. Christine was watching the boys bury Leonardo, but Francine was earnestly drawing a sea creature that looked like it was a dragon.

"See," Patsy said, laughing a bit, like she'd been more concerned than she pretended.

"Help me," Leonardo called out, seeing us standing there, taking in everything. "Patsy, my darling, surely you don't want your husband buried in the sand?"

That propelled Patsy forward, running toward him. The boys stopped a moment to see what she'd do, but she surprised everyone when she started pushing sand into the hole. The boys laughed and sat back to watch. Only Patsy got too close, and Leonardo pulled her down beside him, kissing her with wild abandon that sent the boys into fake vomiting and fascinated peeking.

I was secretly jealous, wanting to do the same with Bonnie but not daring to attempt it. Instead, catching movement from the corner of my eye, I looked up to see the river dragon that Bonnie had spoken of rearing up his huge head to peer down at us.

"Watch out, everyone," I cried out, panicking because the dragon was enormous.

Bonnie stopped working on the castle and paused to look up. "Hey, Claro," she called out, excited to see him again.

I dashed forward, scooping up Tommy and Billy, then pulling them back and away from the river. But Bonnie ran towards him, readying a hug. I pushed the boys toward Sally and bolted forward to save my girl. Only, she didn't seem to be in danger, after all. The dragon was hugging her back. I slammed the brakes and stood there with a dropped mouth.

This place kept getting weirder and weirder.

Danuel

Caralee was still in bed rest, according to Koosk, who had a direct line to Burska and Dokófray. I thought Caralee would argue, but she seemed too tired to dispute it. She closed her eyes and went to sleep before I'd even left the hut. I took Miguel with me. It was time for him to see the waking-up process, and he seemed to want to go. (No messages that day. He was back in baby state, not talking much. He seemed almost as sleepy as Caralee.)

The next batch of kids to awaken were the ones the guys had been directly assigned. I wondered about that, since everyone had pretty much been trading off, the whole community taking care of all the kids. I sent a thought to Miguel on it, but he didn't pat my face and try to send any messages. As I said, he seemed normal that day, less seer and more baby.

First wake-up was for Lance. He got Gabriella, age fourteen, and Dolly, age fifteen. Both seemed shy and entirely intimidated by their surroundings and the story Lance told them. But they accompanied us to the next stop, which was Leonardo's young ones: Nicholas, age eleven, and Diego, age thirteen. I didn't have Caralee's sense of people, but both seemed highly strong and over-active, even in their waking from stasis state. Miguel came alive, giving me a report on the two of them. Diego was a bully, and Nicholas was constantly in trouble. Something told me that Leonardo would have his share of problems with them.

Matthew lucked out with two girls: Daniela, aged nine, and Rebecca, aged ten. Miguel had no warning about them.

So, each of the families now had four kids. We'd see how that developed. Hopefully, the young ones who were awakened the week before would be willing to help out.

I know I should have stayed to help them all get acquainted, but I was worried about Caralee and wanted to return to the hut. Miguel said I should talk to Patsy and Leonardo's boys, but Patsy had Tommy and Billy leaning up against her. Miguel flashed me a picture of him being held by Patsy as I chatted with her two boys, so I carried out the plan.

I have no idea if that meant Miguel wanted to communicate with Patsy. Possibly, it was just so I could chat with the two boys and warn them about bad behavior. But the moment Miguel returned to me after having pledged that, yes, there would be another baseball game with my shoe, I took off, running back to my, hopefully, still sleeping wife.

She was awake, sitting up in bed and nursing Alexandro. She smiled when she saw us. I hoped that part of the smile was for me. Catching my thought, she pulled me down for a big kiss. Miguel laughed and demanded one, too.

Sitting on the bed, my son and I, who'd decided to share his thoughts again, relayed the morning's activities and the revelations about Leonardo's boys.

"Bad boys," Miguel said, trying to clarify his insights.

"Then we'll just have to help Leonardo, won't we?" she said to both of us.

Caralee

Burska always seemed to have her reasons for doing things, but it seemed very unfair that Leonardo, who'd had little experience working with kids, was now in charge of the two most troublesome ones. Would that make him bitter and wanting to quit the program? Not that quitting was a possibility. I had a feeling that Dokófray would never permit that.

When I ran the names and genders through my mind, I was delighted that it was now an equal gender mix — six and six. Females were well represented, although Tommy probably wouldn't get his baseball teams. I stopped suddenly and thought about that. Wow, my thinking was really sexist. Who said that girls couldn't outshine boys in baseball?

The guys did their knock-knocks later in the afternoon, and I got to meet the new kids. The youngest of the new ones was Daniela, then Rebecca and Nicholas, one of the troubled boys, followed by the older one of Leonardo's, then Gabriella, who asked to be called Gabby and Dolly. It amazed me to think that Dolly was the same age as me when the aliens had first come.

Diego, the one Miguel had called a bully, could have charmed a herd spider. He was smoothly polite, but Koosk took two steps closer to me when Diego was chatting about liking to read science fiction books. I wondered what Diego would think about our aliens. Would he like sci-fi up close and personal? I mentioned how we were under the jurisdiction of one of the invading aliens, and his eyes lit up. "Do they have guns?" he wanted to know.

His counterpart, Nicholas, seemed less insincere. His eyes darted about as if looking for something to steal. Good luck with that. I asked him a few questions and got only a sprinkle of answers. I didn't think he felt comfortable. Danuel had long ago cleaned up all the blood, and I'd had a sponge bath, so it wasn't the recent birthing.

Maybe Nicholas didn't like females, but Leonardo hadn't mentioned any problems in his relating to Patsy; I sent a message to Miguel asking for insight. Without even touching my face, he shot back the answer. *He's afraid you're going to want him to read, and he can't.* He was eleven years old, and he couldn't read. My heart went out to him.

I looked out at the others, all waiting their turn at being introduced. "I wish I could hand out books for you to read or toys. I'm so sorry. We don't have stuff like that."

It was like someone had poked him with a pin. The tension flowed out of him, and he started to relax. Unfortunately, it wasn't fair to the others to keep him a moment more.

Next, I met Gabby and Dolly, Lance's two. They seemed pleasant. But I knew girls could be really good on projecting sweetness when they were, in actuality, rotten to the core. I hoped that wasn't true of these two. I didn't pick up any negative vibes. "Either of you like baseball?" I asked.

That stunned them and made Danuel laugh. Neither of the girls had ever played. I told them when I was able to get out of bed, we were going to try throwing Danuel's shoe around and bat it a couple of times. Diego, I noted, sneered. The boy sent a look at Leonardo as if asking why he had to put up with such stupidness. Leonardo shook his head, but he didn't need to. A growl from Speeta alerted Diego that maybe it wasn't a good idea to mock me, at least not with herd spiders standing nearby.

Daniella and Rebecca stepped forward next. "I like baseball," Rebecca said, giving an interested look in Diego and Nicholas' way. Alarm bells sounded in my head. Boy crazy. Put a watch on this one. Daniella asked me about the herd spiders. She wanted to know if she could pet one. "We never had one at our house. My father said they were dirty animals, but they're not really animals, are they? They're arachnids."

"These are herd spiders. They're animals, just like we are."

Rebecca jumped in. "We're not animals. Everything else is an animal, but we're humans."

Oh, dear. That sounded like a great debate. I wondered if we could develop a discussion group.

Dolly moved forward. "We're different but the same," she said. "My father used to say humans were better than animals, but we're not."

Thankfully, Danuel told everyone that the meet and greet was over. He thanked them for being so courteous and said he'd see them later. The guys herded away their charges.

"When are they going to do the co-mingling?" I asked Danuel. I cringed when I realized how that sounded. It wasn't that a list of matings was in the works. I meant only that we'd introduce them to their whole new family and let them move in together as a unit.

"Some of it tonight when it's time to bed down. I'm sending a herd spider to each domicile to make sure everyone is safe. In fact, I think we need herd spiders to make sure there aren't any fights or bullying for a while."

He turned to Koosk. A moment of silence as they stared eye-to-eye, and then Danuel turned back to me. "What did you think? Get any impressions?"

"Yeah. Nicholas can't read. That came from Miguel. It's no wonder he was constantly in trouble. He's been trying to cover it up. Diego is . . . well, I hate to say it, but swarmy. He pretends to be polite, but underneath right now, he's nasty, a festering wound of yickiness."

"Wow, Caralee. Nicely said. Maybe repeat that when we're hungry and out of food."

I laughed. The only other problem is Rebecca."

His face looked puzzled. "What? You picked up something bad about her?"

"She's boy crazy. That isn't uncommon for the age, but it means we have to watch her, especially around King Swarmy. He might take advantage."

"If King Swarmy causes too much trouble, we'll send him up the ship. That should civilize him quickly."

We both laughed, but there was an element of not joking present.

Leonardo

I picked it up right away. I got the lemon in the bunch. Diego. I knew his ilk. It probably reflected off his father. I decided I'd probe that first. Nicholas was slightly off, too, but he was hard to pinpoint. When we took the kids down to the sand, neither Diego nor Nicholas wanted to do such a childish thing, but when Bonnie mentioned the river dragon, they decided that maybe there was something to watch for.

Samuel came over and introduced himself. He seemed like a good kid. But Diego showed that he thought himself better than Samuel. Older, too. Next came Tommy, hoping to recruit for the baseball game. Diego stock his nose in the air like the idea was an affront, which probably meant that Diego didn't know how to play baseball.

"We can't play a real game until we have something more than a shoe to bat around," I said.

Then Diego perked up. "You're stick hitting a shoe?" He laughed, hurting Joey's feelings a bit, but I had to agree that it was pretty funny.

"Any ideas on how to make a baseball?" I asked.

"You need rubber," Christine said.

Diego sneered. "What makes you think I'd want to use a rubber with you?"

"Enough," I snapped. "Christine, the problem is that the only thing we have with rubber is Danuel's shoe."

Ignoring Diego, she looked thoughtful for a moment. "Couldn't you melt the shoe rubber into a ball?"

Smart girl. "That's worth checking on next time we see Dokófray, not that he'd understand the necessity of a baseball."

"The alien?" Diego sneered for about the hundredth time that day.

I shot a glance at Patsy and shrugged. She smiled into my eyes, apparently approving of my progress so far. Okay, I could do this. Project Diego, here I come.

The kids were worn out by the time we left. No river dragon sighting, unfortunately, but there was always the next visit. Daniela was the most upset. She cried because she couldn't stay long enough to wait for the dragon.

We had a supply of fruits back at our hut, so we slipped away Patsy, me, and our four children: seven, eight, twelve, and fourteen. Not even possible, I thought. That would have made Patsy (fictiously) pregnant at three years old. I almost laughed at the joke of it but smothered it, not wanting Patsy to ask what I found so funny. Besides, I was keeping a watch on Diego. An abused child and a kid whose parents and aunt had died didn't need to be bullied. It was my job to make sure that didn't happen. Mine and the herd spider that seemed to be stalking us.

We got inside, and the thing followed us in like he was part of the crazy new family I'd accumulated. "Uh, are you in the wrong place?" I asked him, but herd spiders didn't communicate with me like they did Danuel. The thing just collapsed in a corner and curled up like it had decided to sleep there.

"What are we going to do?" Patsy asked. "That's a male. They have fangs."

She was hanging onto my arm like I was the MAN of the hour. I smiled down at her and reassured her that the thing wasn't about to bite any of us. "He's just here for protection," I said. "Maybe Dokófray sent him to watch over us?"

Diego was back to his sneering again. "Yeah, but they crawl out in the night and eat people. They start with the youngest because they taste the best. Plump and juicy."

I knew I should have cut him off before he got all that out, but I was too busy grinding my teeth. The kid was instant torture. He'd better watch out that I didn't *sic* the herd spider on him.

"No, not so, Diego. Actually, they never eat adults, but they always start with the oldest of the children. There's more meat on them."

Patsy slugged me half-heartedly, then giggled. "You're so funny, Leonardo. You know herd spiders only eat insects."

Tommy and Billy had been big-eyed at first, but they were already laughing again.

"These are our new parents," Tommy said. "Now they're going to be yours, too. And we'll be your little brothers. We're a family, and one day Patsy and Leonardo are going to get married, and we all get to be at the wedding."

Nicholas had been quiet throughout the herd spider discussion, but he chimed in then. "You're not married? Are you living in sin?"

"No," Patsy said, aghast at the idea. "We're just a legal couple, not a real couple. I mean, we will be one day, but not yet. Right now, we're just cooperating."

"Is that what you call it?' Diego grinned with that sardonic, nasty look of his.

That pulled my tug. "Outside, you," I said. "Time for an attitude adjustment."

Panic came over his face then. I realized by his expression that he'd been beaten before. No one gets that look otherwise.

I tugged his shirt and half carried him outside; sorry I had to be so rough, but he'd gone way past my tolerance. It was time to lay down the law.

"Listen, Diego. I'm not about to put up with sexual innuendos. You used one on Christine and now on Patsy. Gentlemen do not talk that way to ladies or young girls. Got that?"

The panic had subsided somewhat, probably because I hadn't grabbed something to whip him with.

"I don't have to listen to you. You're not my father, and I didn't obey him most of the time."

"That's too bad, but you're in a different place now. You have options."

"Options? Like what?" he said, crossing his arms in opposition.

"Option one: You sleep with the herd spider.

"Option two: You go inside and apologize to your new mother, then settle down to sleep through the night without argument.

"Option three: We call Dokófray, and he can take you up on his alien ship.

"By the way, did Danuel tell you about that experience? Three days without food, no water, no toilet. A small room with no door, nothing to do, no way out?"

"That's impossible. There has to be a door."

"Not when aliens can walk through walls."

Diego glared at me a moment, then finally sighed. "You're not going to hit me?"

"Nope. No need."

"But I have to choose one of those options? What if I choose the ship?"

"Then I tell the herd spider. He tells Danuel, and Dokófray comes and gets you."

"What if I choose the herd spider? You said he won't eat me."

"Herd spiders like to wrap at least six of their arms around a person when they cuddle down to sleep. That wouldn't be my choice, but it's up to you."

"Okay, I'll tell Patsy I'm sorry, but I'm not calling her Mom. My mom is dead. I think Dad beat her to death. Maybe."

I poker-faced that. It could be the truth, or it could be a lie. No telling, but I held the door open for him as we entered the hut.

Tommy and Joey had already bedded down. I noticed they'd moved their sleeping reeds closer to Patsy than the previous night. Maybe Diego's words about the herd spider had scared them. Maybe they were already reacting to the fear that Diego might prank them.

Nicholas had spread his reeds on the other side of the two. He wasn't taking chances, either.

Diego marched over to Patsy, then stood there, stubbing his shoe against the dirt floor. "Uh, Patsy. Uh, Leonardo says I need to tell you I'm sorry. My tongue sometimes says things I don't really mean. You're nice and all, so I'm sorry for being rude."

Patsy gave him a big smile. "That is a really nice apology, Diego. Thank you. I'm glad you've joined our family. Your reed is over there. You can park it wherever you feel comfortable."

Diego thought he was being smart when he dragged it over to the door.

"Nope," I said. "The herd spider is not going to let you do that, and neither will I. Find a spot away from the door, Diego."

He turned and looked at me like he was trying to see how far he could go before I erupted, but then he shrugged and dragged his reeds back over next to Nicholas. He plopped down angrily then breathed out a hiss of breath.

I made my way over to the herd spider, figuring I needed to make amends. I was remembering the things Matthew had said about how they were intelligent and how they understood everything that we said.

I sat down next to him. "I'm sorry if I was rude earlier. I'm grateful you're here to help out. I'm new at all this, so I don't really know what to say, but I'd like to make amends. Friends?" I asked. I held my hand out to the spider, not knowing if that was the protocol for herd spiders or if the guy had even understood my words.

"I'm Leonardo, by the way," I added.

The herd spider stared into my eyes for a moment. I felt a pinch at my forehead, A subtle stab, and then a tickle.

Wahbu

It was true. The herd spiders did understand. They had names, too, and communicated if they wished to.

I bowed my head in a brief nod, then headed for my bed reeds. My life has suddenly gotten really complicated: a kid whose father might have beaten his mother to death. A herd spider, Wahbu, who'd spoken to me. A female who might or might not find me worthy . . . It was a dangerous game I was playing. I was probably in over my head, and the truth is I had no idea how to romance a female, and I knew absolutely nothing about child-rearing.

Patsy

I could feel Leonardo worrying, but he'd passed my tests. I wanted to tell him so, to go crawl in next to him on his sleep mat, but we had kids now. Four boys with eyes watching everything we did. So, no smooching between fights. No hugging and maybe . . . No, not going there.

There was a hush in the hut. I could hear four sets of sleep-breathing going on. Did I dare at least go sit with Leonardo?

I stood up and, tiptoed over, and sat down. "You're doing a good job," I said.

His eyes were examining mine, assessing meanings. "Good job with the boys or with you?"

I was glad it was dark in the room. I wanted to bolt away, not cross that bridge of finality, but I also wanted him to know. "I'm learning to trust you, Leonardo. It takes time, but I think you're . . . well, improving."

He sat up, swept me into his arms, and kissed me. Then he picked me up and carried me back to my mat. "It's a good thing we have supervision. I want to do more than kiss you."

He lay me down, then backed away. I was smiling when he left.

I slept hard, warn out by the newness of the past day and by the sun and the sand digging, but I woke to hear Billy whimpering.

"Don't hit me anymore. Please, Dad. Please."

"It's okay, Billy. No one's beating you. Your dad's not here. You're okay."

I opened my eyes to peek. It was Diego with Billy, rocking him back and forth, soothing his fears. I closed my eyes and listened, not wanting to intrude in such a miraculous moment.

"It's going to be okay here, Billy. No one's going to beat you anymore. You're my little brother. I'm going to watch out for you. Okay? Now, close your eyes. No more nightmares. I'm here. Shhh."

I fell back asleep and woke up wondering if I'd dreamed it, but I hadn't. Leonardo was nodding his head as he looked at me. I knew from his expression that he'd heard it, too.

We let the boys sleep in that morning. We were taking another day off to play baseball and to celebrate our new awakened ones.

I again tiptoed over to Leonardo. He swung his arm around my shoulder and kissed me on the cheek. "I like waking up with you," he said, then grinned his mischievous crooked smile.

We stood there like that, not speaking, just admiring our family. I thought then that it was going to be okay. Things were going to work out. At least, I hoped so.

Chapter Eleven

Caralee

Another day, when I was missing all the fun, I thought, but then Dokófray popped in. He gave me a smile, picked up Miguel, checked on the baby, and then tickled one of Danuel's uncovered toes.

My husband blasted up. "Caralee," he bellowed, then saw it was Dokófray. It was totally out of character for the alien. Danuel and I exchanged a shrug and a smile, then looked up to see what he wanted. He was playing a game with Miguel, tossing him from leg to leg, traveling the baby up and down his body, and Miguel was roaring with laughter.

Alexandro, awakened from his night's sleep, was both wet and hungry. Danuel got up and took care of the first, then handed the baby over to me to take care of the second.

"You still tired, Caralee?" Dokófray asked.

"More bored than tired," I said.

Danuel, instead of backing me up, said, "Not true."

"I thought so. I bring plant nourishment. It Boxaff. Burska says it gives energy after baby."

Danuel walked over to take it from Dokófray. "Do we need to find more? How does she eat it — chewed raw or in a liquid?"

"Only this. No more needed. Eat. No liquid."

Danuel handed it to me while I was still nursing. I crunched. It tasted like licorice, or at what I remembered licorice tasting like. One of the visitors from Earth had given me a piece for guarding their bugflyer. I'd started to tell them that no one would bother it, but candy was candy. I accepted it and ate it while I waited by their bug flyer. I wanted to save a piece for my parents, but it was too delicious. Before I knew it, I'd gobbled down the whole piece.

Now, I had something that tasted the same. Maybe not as sweet, but just as tasty. I ate every bite.

"Good. Now, can get up. "No more bed rest, but no baseball game. You watch only."

"How did you know about the game?"

He didn't answer, but he'd brought us a present. It was a genuine softball, or so Danuel said. I didn't know the difference between a softball and a baseball.

"Burska, allow this one thing. She thinks good for children."

"Thank you so much," I said. "Will you stay and watch?" Dokófray's proboscis did the thing, which meant laughter, but he didn't respond. He was gone in that instant, probably still wagging his proboscis.

The practice game went well. There was no loser or winner. Too many kids were just learning how to play the game. Every one of the kids got a shot at hitting the ball and throwing it, including each of the girls, much to Joey's opposition. Then Sally, Patsy, and Bonnie took their turn, and the girls went wild. So, the males had to step up to the bat. In the end, I was the only one who didn't get to play, except Miguel and Alexandro, of course.

The next day, it was back to working on the huts. The older kids helped some, although Danuel said they mainly got in the way, but it was training for the future.

Two days later, Dokófray was back, declaring that it was time to wake up more people. We hadn't even adjusted to the ones we had. The kids were doing better than we'd expected, but that probably just meant that they hadn't had enough time to adjust and feel comfortable enough to make trouble. (I hoped that wasn't negative thinking, but wasn't there an old saying about cougars or lions or some other cat not changing their spots?)

But Dokófray had issued orders, so it was push forward on adoptions. It was decided that some would stay at the village while others would start building a new village, as Danuel called it. The new village would contain young adults and older teens. All the younger children would remain with us, much to the disappointment of Daniella, who was itching to ride a herd spider and hoped that by going to the new village, she would get to ride one there.

But the villages would be close, so close we could walk if we didn't want to ride a herd spider. I thought that was great. After all, we'd probably all be friendly in the end — almost like family, wouldn't we?

I wanted to organize a lottery about who would be going to Village 2 so we'd all have an equal chance when the time came, but Dokófray said, "No and that he and Burska would decide.

Meanwhile, the preparation for the next group of kids had been accomplished. Dokófray said that Leonardo, Lance, Bonnie, and I were the ones ordered to remain behind. The others would be the retrievers, as Danuel put it with a laugh.

I guess it made since that I needed to remain, having two babies to care for, one still nursing, but . . . I hated that Danuel would be gone again. Couldn't someone else take charge? But my gripes were discounted. The group left, and we stayed. End of subject.

When the retrievers returned three days later, the awakened new batch of six had to be interwoven among us. They were assigned mates, as with the original group, and that was that. Susan, Steven, Natalia, Jose, Guadalupe, and Ricardo joined us, all of them eighteen years of age.

And then in two weeks, a group (without me) went out for more children. It was an operation that repeated over and over too quickly, in my opinion, but Burska insisted on it. She didn't want the children to remain in stasis any longer. I understood that, but everyone was working overtime to accommodate the newbies, and the playtime and getting to know each other stopped.

And we were running out of materials, food, and space.

Burska found another setting, and some of the teens/young adults left to start up the new Village 2, taking their children with them. I lost Lance and Sally to Village 2. They would be the leaders of that village. Bonnie and Matthew would probably be heading out to Village 3 soon. They would be leaders of their site, and Dokófray said the dispersal of those in stasis could increase. The goal was to empty the garbage shacks so nobody would be left as a *pretzel stick*.

All the new village people had adopted herd spiders. Most of the people, including the children, had learned to communicate with their spider. Matthew and Bonnie's Daniella was helping with that. She not only had a love of animals but seemed to have developed a rapport for herd spiders. Like Miguel, she could talk to them.

Since the herd spiders wanted to be tied to us in a personal manner, being able to communicate was essential. Daniella helped those who couldn't seem to tap in. She produced working symbiosis so that everyone was happier — both humans and herd spiders.

All of Speeta and Koosk's spider babies had not yet been apportioned out, but Speeta was again carrying an egg sac. There were many mysteries on Burska, but one of the most fascinating was that only Koosk and Speeta seemed able to reproduce. The reason for that was never given to me. Maybe it had to do with his great size. Neither Dokófray nor Koosk would discuss it.

Another question I still came up empty on was the relationship between the herd spiders and the aliens. Why did the aliens look like herd spiders? And why did the aliens stay in orbit, forever following Burska's dictates? The more questions I had, the more the questions mutated and multiplied. Danuel just laughed and said, "Does it matter?"

Anyway, in that way, a year passed, and I found myself pregnant again, but this time, I wasn't the only one. Everyone in the young adult groups had been getting married a la Dokófray's version of marriage. And pregnancies soon followed. Which means there were a lot of walking blimps like me. Doctor Dakowah would be popular.

Our little Miguel was running everywhere, getting in the way, mostly, but Storma, his herd spider, and Nartha, who was Alexandro's, kept the boys safe. The third member of the baby herd spiders from Speeta's huge production, Padora, was waiting for Lissie, who we'd been promised was about to visit. Padora would be going to Butterfly with my little sister.

On Burska, all days were pretty much Paradise-like, except with lots to do, but I began insisting that we have fun time for relaxation. I insisted on baseball day again and sleepovers for the females. The guys started male meeting. Danuel had begun giving them counseling about woman courting techniques, I think, although Danuel refused to give me any details. Also, there was mandatory training given by the aliens on *atmosphere matters* etc.

With pregnancies abundant and dealing with so much, Dokófray and Burska relaxed our schedule even though all the *pretzels* had not been brought here yet. I wondered how many more remained, but Danuel had no idea. There were rooms, he said, that they'd never even entered.

We had lots of good days, days not so good, and horrible ones when everyone forgot about all the aliens' teachings. But the day that Dokófray said my sister was coming, that was a WONDERFUL DAY.

I waited for Lissie with a stomach full of worms. I couldn't sit or stop fretting that something might go wrong. I was afraid her trip would be postponed or cancelled. But it wasn't. She was suddenly dropped into our midst, exactly as Dokófray liked to do it. No sound, no warning. Just there.

I ran, no, I fast walked since Dokófray had forbidden me to run during my pregnancies. In seconds, my sister and I were hugging fiercely. But Dokófray had another surprise. He'd brought my parents, as well. They popped in right in front of me as Lissie had done. Miraculously. The reunion for all of us was teary-eyed.

The newbies (and non-newbies) had all gone to Village 3 to work on huts. No one was around to see my family. It felt strange, but I was glad because it meant that Danuel and I had our family all to ourselves. Selfish, I guess. (Dokófray later explained that had the others seen my special treat, they might have expected visits from their parents. That he said could not happen.)

Dad had finally learned to accept Danuel, and so the two of them did a man hug of sorts, and then Mom was hugging him. Next, everyone greeted Miguel and Alexandro. Dad glowered a bit about me being pregnant again, but he kept his mouth shut, knowing how easily Dokófray could pull the stasis rug over him. After reunion hugs and kisses, we sat down and chatted. I savored having them there and worked on creating new memories. Who knew if I'd ever get another visit, or if I did, when it would be?

Of course, my parents and Lissie chatted with Miguel a bit. He was usually social with everyone, but not so much my parents. As a four-year-old (we calculated,) Miguel rarely stayed still for long, and Alexandro, probably about two and a half, copied him in everything, so Mom couldn't get either of them to sit in her lap.

But Lisse soon had him clinging to her. I think Miguel must have remembered his sister. In a few minutes, the two were sitting in the dirt, drawing pictures. Alexandro, of course, joined in. His drawings were only scribbles, but he was always content when he was near his big brother.

Lissie was six already, no longer the little toddler I remembered. Mom said she was small for her age, but my little sister looked perfect to me. She was tanned from the sun and full of smiles. "She's as healthy as a *Spigling*," Mom added, although I had no idea what a *Spigling* was.

I wondered if Lissie would take off, striding down to the sand area where she'd played so often, but she didn't. She stayed nearby, perhaps realizing her time with us would be short.

"I missed you, Cara," Lissie said, looking up at me as if she felt my thoughts focused on her. Of course, I said it back. Lissie then started gushing about the animals on Butterfly. "The variety and variations among even the same species are phenomenal," she told us. (That reminded me of how much I'd worried about Lissie's language deficiencies as a three-year-old.) No worries now, obviously.

Lissie's eyes lit up when she talked about animals. I figured she must be happy on her Butterfly Planet. Maybe Dokófray and Burska had been right about that decision despite the fact that it had torn Danuel's and my heart in two.

When Lissie finally ran down telling me all about it, her bubble of excitement waning as she looked around, probably wondering where Koosk was, it gave Mom and Dad a chance to talk.

Dad had already been talking with Danuel. I couldn't tell if he'd been scolding Danuel about my pregnancy or not, but if so, Dad better be careful. Dokófray would not like that. But Danuel's forehead was not looking all broody as it sometimes got when the young ones (or Leonardo) started popping off. Danuel had turned into a real adult about all that. He rarely raised his voice, but he did occasionally get glum when the kids didn't see how talking things out made everything flow so much easier.

But he wasn't wearing that face at the moment, so maybe he and Dad had just been talking about hut-making or something else neutral.

Dad had already told us that he was the vice president of Monarch, the main city of Butterfly. He said that the government was expanding and might soon include the second smaller city of Swallowtail. The elections would come in a month, he said, so he'd be campaigning at full throttle for that. (I wondered if a throttle was another of Butterfly's animals, but I didn't ask.) It was obvious that Dad had gotten his wish. Like Lissie he was ecstatic about life on Butterfly.

Mom proudly told me that she was head of the nursing staff. She chatted about the new hospital Monarch was building. Thanks to the arrival of the Earth ship, they had an abundance of resources to supply the building with the latest technological machinery and everything else they could wish for. Mom looked equally happy. Burska had been right to send my parents away.

After hearing about their lives on Butterfly, I finally got the chance to introduce Padora to Lissie. The herd spider went right up to my sister, crooned to her, and stared into her eyes. The two bonded in seconds. Lissie said that Padora was eager to see butterflies, but when Lissie described all the insect life, Padora was even more excited.

Dokófray appeared and sat down with us. (Well, not sat. The aliens just kind of spread their legs out and collapsed, but they called it sitting.)

Lissie deserted Miguel and Alexandro to run over and embrace the Big D, as she was calling him now. Dokófray no longer looked uncomfortable with such things. He hugged her back with all of his legs.

"I planted the trees," she said. They grew a lot. They produce heaps of fruit. And there are lots of insects that come to fight over them. Padora is going to be very happy. Thank you, Big D."

Dokófray nodded, then disengaged himself and stepped back. That's when Lissie saw Koosk. She dashed over and threw her arms around him. She was sobbing loudly by then, her tears splashing. Koosk had never been fond of water, but he accepted it, not pulling away until she'd calmed down. Then his proboscis reached out and touched her face. She giggled.

He'd brought Speeta with him, but I don't think Lissie was interested in meeting the herd spider who had stolen her best friend away. At least she wasn't until Koosk explained that Padora was Speeta and his daughter. Then Lissie perked up. "Padora is part Koosk and part Speeta," she told us, and her smile looked radiant.

Neither Mom nor Dad looked happy to see the giant herd spider. Mom looked fearful. She'd always been afraid of the spiders, even when we'd had a ranch full of them, and none of them had been as big as Koosk. Dad was more familiar with the spiders, but he'd never been as close to them as Lissie. They were her favorite playmates at one time. And then, when Koosk had moved in, she'd probably decided that herd spiders were cooler than people.

Padora introduced herself to my parents. I could tell that Koosk had worked with her on her manners. But even though the spider bowed to my parents and acted humble and as gentle as the domesticated ones we used to train to the saddle, my parents didn't make any effort to act friendly back. They didn't even see how cute and fuzzy she was.

The truth is that my parents might never accept Padora as anything more than a pet for Lissie. I wondered how Koosk and Speeta felt about that. But then, Padora would be with Lissie. Perhaps that would make all the difference. Would they miss Padora? She'd been living in our hut for a long time. She must be close to her parents. Perhaps, as Danuel would say, I was anthropomorphizing, a fancy word that he explained as meaning I thought herd spiders thought just like us. I knew they didn't. Kind of.

(How did Danuel know such a big word? Of course, I asked him that. He told me how Dokófray, finding out that Danuel missed learning stuff, was introducing a new word every time the two met. It was like a game they played. I don't know why I didn't get to play, but Danuel did all his new vocabulary words with me.)

Dad asked to see the new huts that were being built in Village 2 and Village 3, but whatever method Dokófray had used to bring my family to us — he called it the Boomerang Effect — it apparently reversed itself in seven hours. It was instant here, then instant back home again, but *brevity was of the essence*, as Dokófray liked to say.

We had a meal together, my parents eating the fruit although they knew it didn't offer them sustenance. Mom cozied up to the boys and explained how she was their grandma and loved them a whole lot.

Miguel sighed heavily, then patted her on the cheek. "I 'member," he said, but Burska says you can't stay. Be happy. Watch over Lissie. She is my sister."

Mom tried to explain that Miguel had it wrong, but he shook his head. "She is my big sister, Burska's Queen. I know. Burska said so."

I shook my head to stop my mom. I knew she wanted to correct Miguel and probably argue about how a planet couldn't talk. Mom stared into my eyes a moment and said, "Oh."

I got a bit of a lecture then from Dad, a cautious one because Dokófray was standing beside them. Dad told me to be extra careful and ordered Danuel to watch out for me and not let me lift things.

"After this baby, maybe you could give Caralee some time off from baby-making," Dad said, shooting a wary glance at the alien.

Dokófray was watching Lissie and Padora, but I knew he was listening to my parents, monitoring everything. His eyes turned to my dad. They did a moment of unfriendly eye-to-eye. My father was the first to look away.

"Sorry," my dad said, and I knew he was asking Dokófray to forgive him for what he'd just said. "I worry about my daughter. You understand that, right?"

Dokófray softened. He nodded. "We watch Caralee. She is very special. No harm. She lives a long, long life."

Dad cleared his throat. "Good. Thank you."

Dokófray turned his head to watch Lissie again, but she had disappeared. Miguel, too. Thankfully, Alexandro was sitting in my mother's lap. She had finally won him over by giving him a piece of fruit. She'd carried a small pocket knife with her and cut off a piece for Alexandro. He had never seen metal before. I was sure that interested him more than the fruit he was given.

"Danuel," I cried. "Lissie and Miguel are gone."

My dad yelled, "Danuel and I will find them."

I cupped my hands and shouted, "Try the sand," but they weren't there. They were found in the tree that Lissie used to climb when Koosk stood underneath, making sure she didn't fall.

Padora knew. She told Koosk, and he told Dokófray.

That was our excitement before the moment it was departure time. Miguel reclaimed his position beside his little brother, but he looked up at me. "I do not want Lissie to go," he told me.

"Me neither," I said.

"Then I tell Burska . . ."

"Burska makes the decisions. You know that."

His lip pushed out. His arms crossed. I'd never seen Miguel have a temper tantrum. Not once. But he came close. He wanted to. His eyes flooded with tears. He wiped them away.

"Burska says I can see Lissie through Padora's eyes. I will know she is okay, then."

"Will you share with me?" I asked wistfully.

He nodded. Then he hugged me before standing and pulling up his brother. "We must say goodbye, Burska told me. To Grans and Gramps, too."

"Grans and Gramps? When had he heard that? Not from us, that was for sure. I started to follow Miguel back to my parents, but I stopped, closed my eyes, and said, "Thank you, Burska."

Danuel and I stood back, waiting for our sons to say their goodbyes. Then it was our turn. Of course, I cried. My eyes were always leaky faucets, although I wasn't sure exactly what faucets were. Danuel would know. I would ask him later. I thought it might have something to do with windows. Didn't they leak when it rained too hard?

I thought Dokófray would leave with them, but he said he couldn't now that Padora was going with them. I guess the Boomerang had to balance out like the teeter-totter Leonardo had made for the young kids. It didn't work when two hopped on one side, and the other side had only one. Both sides had to balance.

My parents winked out, then Lissie and Padora, the latter with her legs wrapped tightly around Lissie. I wondered why Koosk and Speeta weren't there to say goodbye, but when I looked up on the bluff, I saw them. They didn't wave as we did, but they were watching Lissie and Padora. I wondered if it was as hard on them as it was on me. But they'd had a lot of babies. I had only one sister, mother, and father. Did that matter?

Dokófray promised he'd bring Lissie and her parents back to Burska after I gave birth to the Peacemaker. That would be Baby Angelica, the pregnancy after my current one. So, that was something to look forward to in — what, two or three years? I tried to get an estimate, but, of course, Dokófray was gone, having popped back to his ship.

Dokófray had once told us that one day, Lissie would return to Burska to live. It didn't seem like that would be happening anymore. I was pretty sure that my sister loved Butterfly. That was another question I wanted to ask Dokófray, not that he was good about responding to such queries.

Later that night, it hit me that Mom had mentioned the Earth ship the aliens had sent to Butterfly. "I guess the Earthers decided to stay there," I told Danuel.

"Your father said they crash-landed. No one was hurt, but the ship will never fly again. I wonder how that happened," he said, grinning.

We both laughed, knowing exactly who had caused that and why.

We'd been talking about our visit, entwined as was our usual, but with both boys asleep, we took advantage of the peace of nighttime.

"I love you forever," Daniel told me. "Even enough to confront your father with another baby on the way."

I giggled over that. Dad had looked fierce until he'd shot a glance at Dokófray and decided not to scold Danuel about it again. But my giggles didn't prevent Danuel from deepening his kisses, and that moved us into the really fun stuff.

During the day, we had things to do, but the nights belonged to us, and we savored them deliciously, not cramped at all by my growing belly and two sons, both sleeping on the mat with our two favorite herd spiders.

And so it was on Burska, where four-year-old Miguel was the Spider King and two-year-old Alexandro was the Judge and would soon be followed by the Doctor, the Peacemaker, and the Caretaker.

Danuel and I still didn't know what any of it meant, but that was okay because we'd learned the importance of relaxation mode, the principles of civility, and most importantly, that *atmosphere signifies*.

Coming Soon!

Lissie, The Spider Queen

Book 4 in the

Spider Hopping Series